'Fantastic... As amusing and wise as Tove Jansson's six-year-old Sophia may be, and as entertainingly frank as Jamaica Kincaid's Annie John is, neither competes with Saara, the intense first-person narrator of the opening part of this novel.'

*Literary Review*

'It's not hard to see why *Things that Fall from the Sky* won the EU Prize for Literature. Ahava has created a poignant tale about disrupted lives, ruptured identities, grief on hold, the desire to be understood and the human need for closure.'

*European Literature Network*

'A whimsical and thoughtful rumination on the terrifying randomness that dictates the course of a life... Ahava's rendering of Saara recalls the first-person intimacy of Mark Haddon's *The Curious Incident of the Dog in the Night-Time* (2003) and serves as an example of what strong writers can do with simple sentences.' *Booklist* (starred review)

'A poignant tale about what shapes our identity and choices.'

*The Tablet*

'A literary fairy tale... People who live in cold climates need stories that can be spun and unspun around warm hearths.'

*Literary Hub*

'Ahava embraces the eccentricities of her characters and the role of randomness in the novel's plot, pivoting from a meditation on grief into something closer in tone to the Ricky Jay-narrated prologue of Paul Thomas Anderson's *Magnolia*.'

*Words Without Borders*

'Selja A⸻ ⸻ mind a
fairy ta⸻ and wise
– quite ⸻ *r Zeitung*

©Liisa Valonen

**Selja Ahava** is a novelist and scriptwriter. Her acclaimed debut novel *The Day the Whale Swam through London* (2010) was awarded the Laura Hirvisaari Prize. Her second novel, *Things that Fall from the Sky* (2015), won the EU Prize for Literature and was shortlisted for the Finlandia Prize and the Tulenkantajat Prize.

**Emily Jeremiah**, Professor of Contemporary Literature and Gender Studies at Royal Holloway College, University of London, and **Fleur Jeremiah**, a linguist, are the translators of numerous Finnish novels, including the Man Booker International-longlisted *White Hunger* by Aki Ollikainen.

# things that fall
# from the sky

## SELJA
## AHAVA

Translated from the Finnish by
Emily Jeremiah and Fleur Jeremiah

ONEWORLD

A Oneworld Book

First published in North America, Great Britain and Australia
by Oneworld Publications, 2019
This mass market paperback edition published 2020
Originally published in Finnish by Gummerus Publishers as *Taivaalta tippuvat asiat*

ISBN 978-1-78607-729-5 (paperback)
ISBN 978-1-78607-542-0 (eBook)

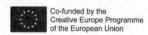

Co-funded by the
Creative Europe Programme
of the European Union

The European Commission support for the production of this publication
does not constitute an endorsement of the contents, which reflects the
views only of the authors, and the Commission cannot be held responsible
for any use which may be made of the information contained therein.

Work published with the support of the Finnish Literature Exchange

FILI FINNISH
LITERATURE
EXCHANGE

Printed and bound in Great Britain by Clays Ltd, Elcograf S.p.A.

Oneworld Publications
10 Bloomsbury Street
London WC1B 3SR
England

MIX
Paper from
responsible sources
FSC
www.fsc.org    FSC® C018072

A BEGINNING is something that does not itself follow
from something else, but after which another event
or process naturally occurs.

A MIDDLE both follows a preceding event and itself
has further consequences.

AN END, by contrast, is that which naturally occurs,
whether necessarily or usually, after a preceding event,
but need not be followed by anything else.

Aristotle, *The Poetics*

# A WALLED-IN GIRL

I

'What's on your mind back there?' Dad asks, glancing in the rear-view mirror.

Our eyes meet.

'Nothing,' I reply.

We turn off at the petrol station. You go right here for Extra Great Manor, left for Sawdust House. These days we mostly turn right.

Adults are always asking what children are thinking. But they'd be worried if they got a straight answer. If you're three and it's a windy day, it's not a good idea to stare at the horizon and say, 'I'm just wondering where wind comes from.' You're better off claiming you're pretending to be a helicopter. And when you're five, don't ask too many questions about death or fossils, because grown-ups don't want to think about dying, or characters in fairy tales getting old, or how Jesus died on the cross. When I was little, I thought

Mum's grandma was a fossil, because she died a long time ago. But these days I know you can get fossils with ferns, snails or dinosaurs in them, but not grandma ones. Or human ones, for that matter.

A grown-up will see a child sitting in the back of a car and think she's counting trucks or the letters on road signs, or pretending her fingers are princesses, but, actually, she might be thinking about the outline of a grown-up, or time.

I've considered time a great deal. I have grey cells in my brain. I use them to think about how time marches forward and heals. Grown-ups say time heals and that means that when time passes, what's happened changes into a memory and you remember it less and less clearly. When you can hardly remember it at all, you've been healed.

But I don't want not to remember Mum. I want to remember Mum properly, without the aeroplane, without the shards of ice, without the hole in the porch. The way Mum was normally.

*MUM NORMALLY. Mum wanders around wearing furry slippers and Dad's big jumper. Mum makes a nest for me in the corner of the sofa using a quilt, and wraps me up in it before going to get firewood from the woodshed. Then she gets me dressed for the day in front of the stove. First she opens the stove doors, warming the clothes near the flames and shaking the chill off them, before undressing and then dressing me as quickly as possible. Mum shovels snow, wearing a blue bobble hat, and clasps a mug of tea to get the cold out of her hands.*

*That's what Mum's like normally.*


Dad says time-heals is a load of shit. According to Dad, the only people who say that don't understand anything about anything. They've never been through anything. And my grey brain cells think Dad may be right because, at least so far, nothing's healed, even though the summer holidays have already started.

And so I sit on the back seat and say 'nothing' and think about the healing power of time. To be on the safe side, I decide to remember Mum every day, before time has the chance to do too much healing.


The car's windscreen wipers sweep across the glass, and our damp clothes make the window mist up. Dad drives into a puddle at full speed; he likes the way the water whooshes up the sides.

It's raining.

It's always raining, these days. At school the teacher says, 'Hey, we're not made of sugar.' We put on waterproof trousers, raincoats and wellies and go outside. I think of sugar children, melting in the rain. Just sticky, sweet waterproofs left behind in the schoolyard.

Back in Sawdust House, Dad was always worrying that the roof would leak and he'd notice too late and by then, the attic would be rotting. Mum always said Dad was a drama queen, the way he made such a big deal out of things, ordinary things.

But these days, everything is a big deal. And Dad barely notices the rain. These days, Dad can saw branches in the rain and get soaking wet, and all Auntie says is: 'Let him slog it out for a bit.'

These days, I get picked up from school every day by car. When we were still living in Sawdust House, Mum only came to get me if it was raining. After a working day, Mum would smell of cigarettes. She'd have pins in her shirt collar and paint on her fingers, and her hair would be twisted up in a work bun.

*MUM WORKING. Mum's workplace is underground. It smells of dust, tobacco and old clothes, and it's packed full of stuff from floor to ceiling. Mum has big golden scissors which she uses to cut cloth, and a velvet pillow covered with pins on her wrist. She has one long nail, which she uses to draw in the folds of the fabric precisely. A pen sticks out of her work bun.*

*No one's allowed to touch Mum's scissors. Mum hangs the scissors on a hook for the night.*

*That's what Mum's like at work.*

## 2

At last, the car turns into the avenue that leads to Extra Great Manor. I put an end to my thinking, draw a white line around the pieces of Mum. When I stop my thoughts like that, I can pick them up at a later point, from the same spot.

I love this straight, tree-lined lane. When you turn into it, you find an ancient road suddenly lying before you. A velvet curtain opens, the light changes, music strikes up. Violin music. The team of horses runs; the driver's cloak billows. At the end stands Extra Great Manor.

Once a house is old enough, it stops looking man-made. It becomes alive, just like a mossy stone or a magnificent old tree. I imagine Extra Great Manor rising from the ground like a mushroom. First, a stone ring appeared. Then, a red figure rose from inside it and solidified to become walls. As time passed, wooden planks stretched and windows opened. A tower sprang up, and the roof grew stronger. Moss mottled the stone foundations, and the colour of the walls faded. That's how Extra Great Manor was born.

Oaks and maples arch above us, forming a green tunnel, and the sand crunches. It's a bit like we're entering a magic wood or a time tunnel. Time splits, and the manor house appears ahead.

'Dad, slow down.'

You need to arrive slowly at places like this. Before, gentlefolk came with their horses, and there was a stable especially for visitors.

Auntie's sheep are standing on the lawn in front of the main steps, on the posh side. There are eight white ones and three black ones. When people call sheep black, they really mean brown, in the same way they say fish swim when what fish really do is dive.

Bruno is the tamest of Auntie's sheep. Whenever I go over to him, he says baa and puts his head against my thigh. He can't push me over yet; an adult sheep could knock me over with a single shove. Sheep have hard skulls.

Bruno is tame because when he was little, I fed him with a baby bottle. Now he thinks I'm his mum, and when I walk past, he always comes up to the fence and bleats. Bruno is black, which really means brown, and one of his ears hangs down lower than the other one, because his mum tried to bite it off. Even if a lamb has just come out of its bum, a sheep might not realize who its baby is.

Bruno was sure he wanted to live and he latched on to the baby's bottle like a wild beast. Milk splashed everywhere, the bottle bubbled and Bruno's mouth slurped and smacked. Looking down at him, you could see his tummy getting bigger as it filled with warm milk. It wasn't a cute job, feeding Bruno. It wouldn't look nice in a children's book, the way my hands got wet with milk, holding the bottle.

Bruno can eat grass now.

Today the sheep look miserable: no one's saying baa. They're lying all over the grass, feet tucked firmly under their bellies. They always lie in the same gangs. The brown ones are friends and the white ones form two different groups. They look at each other as if they don't get what the others are doing in the same pen.

When it's raining hard, the wool of the sheep goes flat and they look thin and wet. Auntie said that if you throw a sheep into water, it sinks.

There's smoke coming out of the small chimney of Extra Great Manor, which means that Auntie Annu has lit a fire in the kitchen. That's good because otherwise the kitchen is so cold you don't want to take your coat off.

I know that you mustn't complain of the cold if you live in a manor house.

## 3

When I was six years old, Auntie Annu got seven numbers right in the lottery. A genuine Double Mega Jackpot was up for grabs: so much money it's hard to put into words. It's more than the African Star in the board game: the diamond that's worth more than the rubies and all the notes put together. When you win, you have to rethink things a bit. For example, do you enjoy working? Do you want to carry on playing African Star? Do you want to live in a different place, or sign up for riding lessons, or buy diamonds? Then you have to consider what's important in life. Family, of course, but that's got nothing to do with money. Anyway, Auntie Annu doesn't have family because she's got no kids. Also, you've got to beware of burglars. Even if you have won the lottery, you might not get to go into space, and money can't buy happiness, and you won't get to have servants in your house.

We went to Auntie Annu's for a Double Mega Jackpot Coffee, and on the way there in the car, Mum and Dad explained that the lottery win was a secret not to be shared in nursery or at my friends' houses or in the shop or on the bus. We were the only ones who knew – that's why Auntie had made a gateau. This was a secret celebration. I like celebrations and secrets and cakes.

*MUM DRESSED UP. Mum has a silk dress with black and silver on it. Mum is tall, because she's wearing high heels. Her hair forms a swirling peak, as if an ice-cream machine had sucked it into the clouds. Dad looks at Mum, smiling. His chest swells as he tries to stand as tall as Mum. Mum's wrist clinks. It seems her hands don't know what to do with themselves, with no hair to push out of her face.*

*That's what Mum's like dressed up.*

I wondered what Auntie would look like now, but she looked just like her old self, only with red hair again. Auntie Annu only went to the hairdresser's when she got a grant or sold a big enough wall hanging. In between visits, her hair went back to normal. She was a big, strong woman, but sometimes she'd be too shy to look you in the eye. She spoke softly, though she had man's hands. Soap, water and textile dust had made Auntie's hands rough and red, and sometimes they were so dry, wounds opened up on the knuckles. They were bear's paws. You could even see the muscles between her fingers.

We crowded into Auntie Annu's flat. It only had one room, plus a kitchen hidden inside a cupboard. The hall was so narrow and so full of coats and shoes that you had to form a queue to get inside, and Auntie Annu had to flatten herself against the door of the toilet in order to let her visitors pass. We threw our coats on top of a dresser. The whole hall was chock-a-block.

Mum, Dad and Auntie Annu hugged and sighed: well I never, I mean really, who'd have thought, what can you do.

'Where's the Jackpot Cake?' I asked.

Auntie Annu winked and drew me into the room.

Auntie's desk had been moved to the middle and a large platter had been placed on top of it. The platter was covered with a tablecloth, coffee cups and saucers, along with the world's finest gateau, a raspberry and white chocolate cream cake. The whole surface was decorated with rolls of liquorice, raspberry pillows, grapes, chocolates, gummy bears, popcorn and marshmallow hearts. A paper umbrella, a shiny swizzle stick, a marzipan rose and a candle were stuck in the middle. Looking at that cake, I saw that the Double Jackpot really was something to write home about. And Mum laughed till she cried. But Auntie must have laughed enough already, because she started setting up folding chairs for Mum and Dad, sniffing a little.

There was no sign of the lottery win.

'You don't take it home,' Auntie Annu explained. 'It went straight to the bank.'

'Would it fit in this room?'

'I'm not sure.'

'Didn't you get to see it?'

Auntie shook her head and clasped her hands together. Then she shrugged.

'Would it fit in a bathtub?'

'It might have been a good idea to go and see it, actually,' Auntie Annu said.

Dad opened a bottle of sparkling wine, and I got to pour myself a mixture of Jaffa and Coca-Cola without prompting a word of criticism from any of the grown-ups.

'Well, then, congratulations, millionaire!' Dad said, and we clinked glasses.

'Well, yes. What can I say?' Auntie said. 'I'll get appointments with the dentist and the gynaecologist right away!'

And the grown-ups laughed again and wiped their eyes.

Then Auntie picked up the cake slice and said, 'You choose, Saara. Where d'you want me to cut?'

And I went for gummy bears, popcorn and the marzipan rose.


Auntie Annu gave some thought to the decision to buy the manor house near our home. It was pink and old, and Auntie Annu had always seen it across the fields when driving our way. It was called Great Manor, but Dad began calling it

Extra Great Manor, because it was so big, whereas Auntie was so small, and no one really needs fifteen bedrooms. Soon everyone else called it that too.

Extra Great Manor had been vacant for twenty years. Before that, it had housed an office; before that, some sort of depot; before that, a children's summer camp. Before that, there had been a war, and the hospital maternity ward had come to Extra Great Manor to escape the bombs. Before that, the manor-house furniture had been sold off at auction, and before that, Extra Great Manor was occupied by a Mrs Gyllenhök, whose grandfather had the place built for his family in 1877.

Auntie Annu moved out of her flat and became lady of the manor. The whole of Auntie Annu's old home would have fitted into the blue parlour of Extra Great Manor, and when Auntie's furniture was carried in, the pieces squatted in the corner of the hall, hopelessly low, tatty and fragile.

The old wooden dresser was the only item of furniture that suited Extra Great Manor. It had stood, dark and heavy, in Auntie's studio, partially hidden behind a door. There wasn't enough room to open its own doors fully. But even stuck in that corner, the cupboard had managed to look like the only real piece of furniture in the flat. Now, as it was carried into the drawing room, it puffed up its chest, straightened itself out and let its decorative patterns flourish.

I loved Auntie's Czech coffee cups. Each one was different, and yet they went together. They had roses of different colours, landscapes, golden whorls, slender blades of grass, rust-coloured hearts and green triangles. The cups hung on the hooks in the cupboard, the matching saucers sitting underneath.

When it was time for coffee, Auntie Annu let me lay the table and choose the cups I wanted. Usually I picked a rose or a circle of girls in folk costume for myself, bear paws or violets for Mum, golden trees or pale-blue sailing boats for Dad, and an extra-large mug that showed a girl in a bonnet feeding Bambi for Auntie Annu.

Extra Great Manor had a thick stone foundation, large steps leading up through a glass veranda, two columns in front of the door and one tower. The manor stood on the ground as sturdy as an oak. You could crawl into the stone foundation through three hatches, but because it had no windows, it was pitch-black inside. There was a circular lawn in front of the manor, on the posh side, and a tree-lined avenue led to it. The tower at the south end had a small summer room at the top, which was reached via a spiral staircase. This granted a 360-degree view, and Auntie Annu arranged for a bed to be carried to the middle of it. The bed had to be lifted through the window in two pieces, using a rope, because the spiral staircase was too narrow. That's where Auntie slept, at the top of the tower, until the nights grew cold.

Downstairs was a kitchen and five rooms all named after colours: Blue, Green, Lilac and Yellow Rooms, along with

Red Hall. Upstairs was a library and fifteen small bedrooms. The bedrooms held metal hospital beds and small, wartime stoves, but otherwise they were empty. There were no books in the library, but a large, old bookcase was discovered in the attic, and Annu, Dad and Mum carried it back into the library together. Auntie later bought a sofa, a smoking table and armchairs at auction.

As soon as she'd moved into the manor house, Auntie Annu bought a flock of sheep. A fence was put up on the posh side to make a pasture for them, and because the fountain pump was broken, the basin became their trough. The sheep were Auntie's lawnmower. Their enclosure was moved to different sides of the house as necessary.

Extra Great Manor breathed. There was room for everything, everything went together and you could open the doors wide. The rooms looked cosy even without furniture, but every now and then Auntie would buy something, like a chandelier.

When winter came, the timber walls gradually surrendered to the chill. The windows frosted over, though there was lichen between the panes. It was cold in the manor house. Auntie closed off most of the rooms and retreated to live in one downstairs corner, to avoid heating the whole house. She made up a winter bed for herself in the Yellow Room and lived just there and in the kitchen. You went into the house via the kitchen door. The Red Hall, the other downstairs rooms and the upstairs became a cold store. Auntie Annu sealed the doors with wool and taped up any gaps. Finally, she hung woollen blankets and old quilts in front of the doors and carried all the wool rugs into the Yellow Room.

People said Auntie was crazy to live in a place like that in winter without proper heating. She should install a heating system, or at least hire a caretaker to clear the snow. But Auntie liked heating up the tiled stoves, and claimed it was handy to be able to store milk on the floor.

In spring, the manor house groaned and creaked. The warmth brought the timbers to life and got the house's blood circulating. It sounded as if someone were walking about all the time. This didn't scare Auntie Annu. 'Extra Great Manor is just stretching its limbs,' she'd say. The groaning and creaking went on till warmth spread throughout the structure. Then the house settled down and the sound of steps upstairs went away.

When a house is young, you have to look after it as if it were a child. It needs adjusting, patching up, care and maintenance. But when a house is, say, two hundred years old, it can look after itself. Everything that's inclined to rot has already rotted. Everything that's inclined to sink and split has already sunk and split. You just have to live in it nicely, which means living as people have lived there before.

Extra Great Manor was slow and old. Its timbers lagged behind the seasons, a bit like the weather on the coast, which is levelled out by the sea. The summer heat was retained until November, and the July heatwaves were well on their way before a stagnant warmth fell into the rooms. Auntie Annu adapted to the rhythm of the house. She put on a woolly jumper and slowed down. She drove to the shop once a week, chatted to the sheep once a day, drank a cup of cocoa at eleven o'clock. After cocoa, she walked once through the downstairs rooms, standing for a moment in every one. Auntie Annu enjoyed the empty spaces; she didn't miss furniture. She no longer had to flatten herself against the door of the toilet when someone came to call.

# 4

We were roped in to help, the day Auntie Annu became lady of Extra Great Manor. Even though no one was moving out of the property, we removed more things from it than we carried inside.

All of Auntie's possessions fitted into one van. But we took out all the furniture that had belonged to the office, the children's summer camp or the warehouse – and that was a lot. The only things Auntie Annu saved were the upstairs hospital beds. Every bedroom contained one or two metal beds that moved on wheels and had sides you could raise. These made Dad shudder, because he had had his appendix removed when he was nine, but Auntie Annu found them atmospheric.

The evening of moving-in day, Auntie Annu whispered to me, 'Come, Saara, I've got something to show you.'

We climbed the stairs to the first-floor landing. Two passages led in different directions. We went into the west passage. Auntie opened the third door we came to.

Behind the door was an unoccupied bedroom, with a bed and two old wooden chairs. Through the window, you could see the front lawn, the fountain, the van and a pile of cardboard boxes. But Auntie walked to the wall on the left-hand side.

'Look,' Auntie Annu said. Gripping the upper edge of the middle section of wall panelling, she gave it a yank.

'A secret door!' I whispered.

And indeed, the panelling slid aside soundlessly. There was a small room behind the secret door, large enough to take a person. Auntie let me try opening the door. You could feel the small pin at the top of the board with your fingers. You had to flick this to the left. Then you heard a gentle click and the panel opened.

We entered the secret room. Auntie had put two velvet cushions and a wool rug on the floor, so it was nicer to sit on. The rear wall had a small window in it. It didn't let in much light, because it was covered by a thick creeper.

'From the outside, you can only see the creeper,' Auntie said.

I had never been in a real secret room before. I had never been to a manor house before, either, and now, suddenly, Auntie had moved into a fairy-tale castle.

Because the secret room seemed like a good place for talking about secret things, the sort you couldn't mention at nursery, on the bus or at friends' houses, I decided to ask Auntie Annu:

'Auntie, how did you know the Double Jackpot numbers?' To be on the safe side, I said it quite softly.

Auntie Annu nodded, thought for a moment and then looked me in the eye. 'It was pure chance.'

'Then why can't you talk about it, if it was chance?'

'That's precisely why,' Auntie Annu said. 'It's so hard to explain.'

We listened to the noises coming from downstairs. Mum was washing up in the kitchen, and Dad was in the hallway, making a racket in the middle of all the piles of boxes. You heard more clatter in the manor house than in the block of flats, because Auntie let us wear shoes indoors. This was because it was moving-in day, but also because the floors were so cold and the stairs were all splintery.

'Saara! Saara! We'll be going in a minute!' Mum's voice echoed up the chimney flue and through the bedroom stove.

I looked at Auntie Annu, who nodded, meaning we ought to go back downstairs.

We stepped silently out of the secret room and shut the wall panel.

'Can we keep this as our secret?' I whispered to Annu.

'Sure,' Auntie replied.

Then we went back downstairs.

I felt good all evening, because now I had a lady of the manor for an aunt, and I was the only one who knew about the secret room in the wall.

# 5

*MUM NAKED. You can see light through Mum's thighs as she scoops hot water from the cauldron in the sauna. Mum has long legs, and her knees click every time she bends them. Mum doesn't have hairs on her thighs like Auntie Annu.*

*Mum stews on the sauna bench, smelling of coconut. She has coconut-scented conditioner in her hair. Mum's back is curved. One of her ankles dangles in the air, and she makes it go round and round and round. I pretend I'm a troubadour and draw my finger along the folds on Mum's tummy as I sing the sounds: plonk plonk plonk plink!*

*A long scar runs across Mum's tummy. That's where I came out.*

*That's what Mum looks like naked.*

Dad went to the sauna alone in Sawdust House, because he found it easier to breathe that way. Mum talked too much in the sauna, about things that were too serious, and she also forgot to ask if it was OK before throwing more water on the stove. Mum threw three ladlefuls of water on at once and then ran into the snow. Dad couldn't stand that sort of thing.

Sometimes, when we sat on the bench, just the two of us, I tried to touch Mum's breasts. Then Mum would slap my hand.

'I did it when I was a baby.'

'That was different,' Mum answered.

'Just this once,' I pleaded.

'No.'

One of Mum's nipples sagged because I sucked it too hard when I was a baby. The other one was normal.

# 6

Time passes, and Mum moves backwards. Trousers and long, straight hair: that's all you can see of her now. A breeze lifts her hair. One hand's holding a cigarette; the other's supporting it. Mum smokes, and moves into the distance.

When Mum leans over the bed, her hair spills out from behind her ears and touches my face, along with her kisses. When I say Mum leans, she's still here. When Mum leaned, she's already going. Dad doesn't talk about Mum, because he can't say leaned. He can't talk Mum into the past; every now and then, he starts a sentence with Mum's name, but he stops halfway.

Mum stopped halfway.

Dad does talk about Mum's belongings, because they still exist. 'Hannele's skis are in the cellar,' Dad will say, in a completely normal voice. 'The cupboards Hannele painted.' 'It's there, by Hannele's boots.'

You can draw a line round a real person, just as detectives do when there's a corpse on the floor. It's easier to understand death when it's got an elbow and a knee and its own place on the floor. And when the dead body is carried away, only a white outline remains: no one left within it. A bit like a lottery win, which would be easier to grasp if it were a pile of money. But memories have no bodies.

In a film, memories appear in black and white.

A person is left standing by the roadside, the car drives off and you can see the person dwindling and disappearing altogether through the rear window. That's the way they die in films.

But it doesn't really look like that. Time doesn't make Mum dwindle, nor do the colours fade. Mum just explodes into pieces and the pieces remain floating in the air. All the fragments are clear – hair, fingers, chuckle, furrows in the skin, nostrils, clicking knees, stomach rumble – but Mum herself is missing.

# 7

'*Everything has the air peaceful. The sun, it is shining; the sea,
it is beautifully blue. But you forget,* mon ami, *that evil always
dwells among us. And this particular individual, this cold-hearted
creature, this assassin, he was especially cunning. He crept into the
library after the others had gone to bed and waited behind the door
till the maid had cleared the table and Monsieur Bowles returned.
Et puis – he stabbed him in the back with a dagger, in cold blood!
He hid the dagger inside a jacket he had left in the room earlier,
and departed. Because he knew he'd be back in the morning; after
all, he'd be the first to be called to the scene! Doctor – or should I
use your real title, you unhappy, bitter orphan, who swore revenge
while still young? – you killed Mr Bowles, you framed Mr Parker,
you pretended to everyone you were a doctor. But you could not
pull the wool over my eyes!*'

Every Sunday, we – Dad, Mum and me – sat down to
watch our favourite Belgian detective on television. Really,

the programme was too scary for children, but we had fewer rules than at my friends' houses, because as a child, Dad had lived abroad, and for Mum, the only rule had been: don't get lost in the forest.

It was the only programme all three of us liked. Dad liked the scenery, because England was the country where he and Auntie Annu had lived as children. Mum wanted to guess who the murderer was, and she guessed wrongly on purpose, coming up with totally wild plots. I liked the final scene, when everything became clear.

In the show, the detective doesn't run or shoot. But he still wins. He remembers the tiniest details, which pass others by. He can spread them out in his mind to form a picture, and he can combine and shift them into different positions. Finally, he fills in all the gaps. That's how he knows the identity of the murderer at the end.

The final scene was always the same. 'Bon, *it is time to reveal the truth. Let us go, Hastings,*' he said, throwing a serious glance at his friend. And every time Hastings appeared as puzzled as the last time.

Mum cried out, 'Parker! It's Parker!'

Dad and I shushed her.

The guests were all summoned into a single room, usually the library or the living room. There was always a suitable number of them. Not too many, because then they wouldn't have all fitted into one room at the same time and the final scene would have been spoiled. Not too few, because then it would have been too easy to guess who the murderer was.

The guests always had secrets, some of which were linked to the murder and some of which weren't. And everything always happened in one place, like a manor house, a train or a small village. The detective wouldn't have had the energy to run around a big city.

Then he started his final speech. Point by point, he revealed how everything had happened.

Sometimes the murderer tried to escape, sometimes they cried or started shouting furiously, sometimes they removed their disguise, but in the end, they were always caught.

'Oui, bien sûr, mademoiselle. *I know everything,*' he declared, patting the young woman's hand. '*And now, let us drink a glass of blackcurrant juice. Mrs Parker assures me it is England's finest.*'

'Parker would have been so much better,' Mum said.

'I bet this was filmed in Cornwall,' Dad said.

I was silent, content, because, once again, everything had been resolved. The lies had been exposed; the show was over. Objects and events had their meanings, and every character their purpose. Nothing was left dangling.


*MUM'S FINGERS AND TOES. Mum has long, dry fingers which smell of cigarettes. Her nails are oval, and there is a ragged wave in her thumbnail. Mum's fingers sit inside her sleeves when she's cold and in her hair when she's thinking. Mum's big toes are* slanted. In summer, Mum wears open-toe sandals, and she paints her toenails blood red.

'Look, Mum's toes have been cut off,' Dad says, but it's a joke. That's what Mum's fingers and toes are like.

# 8

We used to live at Sawdust House. It was our home. It was yellow and white with a red roof. Mum and Dad bought Sawdust House when I was a baby. It had an upstairs, a downstairs and a cellar. At first, the upstairs was cold and old, but we gradually moved up there as well, and I got a room of my own. The heat from downstairs rose upstairs, and the cold air from upstairs flowed into the downstairs hall.

Everything in Sawdust House was a work in progress. Every time someone came to visit and Mum showed them round, she would always say either what things had been like or what they would be like one day.

'There used to be a wall and a door here,' she explained in the hall. 'I've got the wallpaper ready for here,' she said upstairs, where the walls were covered only by raw timbers and shreds of old yellow backing paper. 'There used to be a balcony here, before that new extension. You could make this into two rooms if you wanted to.'

Mum didn't even realize what the house really looked like. Sometimes, when we looked at photos that showed, say, windows with no flashings, electricity cables dangling like Christmas wreaths, old wallpaper half torn off the wall, or other unfinished things, Mum would exclaim: 'How awful, just look at that wall! When will that get done? I do have new wallpaper ready and waiting...'

Our home was called Sawdust House because its walls were filled with sawdust. Every time Dad did some work, he was showered with sawdust. When you slammed the cellar door, out scattered a handful; when a doorway was widened, out spilled a sackful. Sawdust rested on top of the ceiling lights and on the attic floor. It even buzzed around in the cooker fan.

All the sawdust was collected. It was shovelled into sacks and poured on to the attic floor. Dad said that the attic was the woolly hat of the house and the sawdust kept us warm.

Every now and then we had renovation days. Then Mum and Dad ate their breakfast standing up and no one could spare the time to be with me. Often no one even remembered to make cocoa. On a renovation day, it was cold inside because both downstairs doors were open, and Mum and Dad walked in and out with pieces of bread in their hands.

Once, all the things in the living room were carried into the kitchen. The whole of the downstairs had suddenly shrunk and two rooms had been squeezed into one: dining table, sofa, cheese plant, fridge, armchairs, dresser and TV had all been sucked into one room, where you barely had space to walk.

By contrast, the living room had grown. It was so big it echoed. I wanted to dance, but Mum and Dad said no. Mum said I should watch TV, but the remote control had gone missing and the TV was stuck on channel five, so I was allowed to dance a bit before work started.

Only the bookcase stood in its plastic wrapping in the middle of the living-room floor. The bookcase had always leaned against the same wall, and now it seemed as if a piece of the wall itself had been moved to the centre of the room and packaged in white plastic, making it ghostlike. Behind the bookcase, yellow wall was revealed. Elsewhere in the room, the walls were pale brown, but you could see patches of yellow where shelves, pictures and the dresser had been unscrewed and taken away, leaving sharp shadows. The shadow of a shelf, the shadow of a dresser, the shadows of three pictures. I stared in amazement: I had never realized there was so much wall behind the furniture!

Dad stroked the wall with his hand and twisted nails out of it with a hammer. The shelf screws had left big holes, as had the curtain rails and windowsills.

Then Dad unscrewed the wall sockets.

'Dad, you're going to die!' I shouted, because you're not allowed to touch electrical things, especially not with anything sharp.

'It's OK,' Dad said.

He beckoned me over. We looked together at the socket cover as it came off.

You could see inside the wall underneath, where there was a secret passage for electric wires. A brown and a blue lead ran there. The socket contained a metal plate, small screws and other metal parts.

'That's a bit like the socket's skeleton,' Dad said.

I know about skeletons because I've read a skeleton book. An earthworm hasn't got a skeleton, but a snake has. But an earthworm does have a ladder. And I thought, the wires are the house's veins, because they run inside the walls, from one room to another.

Mum stroked the wall, found another nail and twisted it out with the hammer. Then she said, 'Saara, come and stand against this wall.'

And I went and stood where the dresser had stood before. Mum took a thick felt-tip pen out of her pocket and drew a line just above my head. Next to the line, she wrote: 12.5.2007.

'Stay there,' Mum said. 'Don't move.'

She started drawing a line round me. She started next to my shoulder, drew down along my arm, tickling me in the gaps between my fingers, then curved into the armpit and down the side as far as the floor. Then up along the other

33

side. The pen smelled; it had spirits in it. Children aren't allowed to touch them because they won't ever come off. Or child. I'm an only child. Finally, Mum drew round my hair. Two plaits and bobbles. When the felt tip came back to my shoulder, Mum said, 'That's it, now you can jump out.'

And I jumped out and looked at my picture in the middle of the living-room wall. It was like Peter Pan's cut-out shadow in the film. Feet planted slightly apart, shirt tails swinging.

'If someone moves in here after us and they do the house up, they'll find this and see what kind of girl used to live here.'

'Oh, where are we moving?' I asked.

'Nowhere.' Mum laughed. 'We'll never move from here! We've got too many projects to finish.'

Dad laughed, though it didn't sound like a laugh. Then he wrote *Saara* next to the picture Mum had drawn.

'Oh, but aren't you big?' Mum sighed, looking at me and the picture in turn. 'Are you really that big?'

'You did draw round the edges,' Dad said, but he sounded surprised himself.

I went to stand next to the picture, to prove the point.

Then I went to get my own felt tips and coloured in the picture's clothes: turquoise tights and a stripy top. I also drew eyes, cheeks, a mouth and hair bobbles. I thought, this is what's best about renovation days! Bread eaten standing up, sharp objects pushed into sockets, walls decorated with felt tips and space to dance in the living room.

Mum and Dad started on a panelling job. Dad sawed planks in the backyard and Mum carried them in through the porch door. Dad used a spirit level, a tape measure and a pencil; Mum just her eyes and a hammer. After three planks, they started on a renovation argument. Though Mum and Dad always did renovation work together, they always thought the other one did it wrong. This time Mum started it because she thought it was stupid to use a spirit level in an old wooden house where all the floors, walls and corners were all wonky anyway. Dad thought Mum didn't do anything properly and never finished anything she started, leaving him to patch up all her unfinished jobs. The quarrel was always the same, because neither of them changed their way of doing things. This time Mum was annoyed just because Dad had recently bought a new spirit level.

Even so, we had new, light, wood-panelled walls by the evening. No one had the energy to look at them properly, though, because it was dark in the room by then and everyone was too tired. But in the morning, Mum came downstairs and saw Dad had tidied up before going to bed. Mum smiled at the new white walls, and inside the wall, in my tights and a stripy top, I smiled, too. Then Mum decided to make pancakes for the whole family.

*MUM IN THE MORNINGS. In the mornings, Mum wears glasses and she walks straight to the coffee machine. She only goes for a* wee once she's pressed the button. Her thin dressing gown billows as she crosses the living room and opens the curtains. Mum opens the window, or, if it's a warm summer morning, the porch door, and says, 'Ah.'

That's what Mum's like in the mornings.

# 9

In fairy tales, maidens are confined, and then a birch tree grows out of the wall. Mum told me it once happened in real life.

There's no room for maidens in the sawdust walls. Once, I found a handmade wooden boat in the sawdust in the attic, and another time, a salt cellar shaped like a girl, and I've pushed apple seeds into a crack in the wall, but nothing grew from them.

Having peered beyond a socket, I knew that even though nothing grew from the seeds, all sorts of other things go on inside walls. There are passages, and wires snaking from downstairs upwards, and from one room to another, a bit like veins. The wires are brown and blue, and they run between light switches, sockets and lamps, and they're dangerous because you can pierce them with a drill. There are red and blue water pipes, too, and they can freeze even if they are red.

Apart from electrical wires, the sawdust walls contain old doorways and the ghosts of cupboards, and you can find out where they are by knocking. They're a bit like the scars of the house. In the hall wall you can see where the house ended, once upon a time – now, the passage to the bathroom starts here. Upstairs, you can see a door-shaped panel – you used to get to a balcony that way. The wallpaper tears where the doorways are, because winter makes the chipboard sheets shift.

Once, Dad got red spots on his thighs and he thought we had brought back bedbugs from our holiday. He took all the mattresses, quilts, pillows and clothes into the sauna and turned the heat up. He sprayed large quantities of insect poison into the cracks in the bedroom walls and floor and smeared the bed legs with a thick layer of Vaseline. The mattresses baked in the sauna all that day and night, and groggy spiders crawled out of the walls, staggering along the wallpaper and dropping on to the bare bases of the beds. Mum was furious with Dad. No bedbugs were ever found.

*MUM'S VOICE. When Mum's fuming, her voice comes up from her tummy and her whole chest rings out. Once, she managed to prise fighting dogs off each other, she shouted so loud.*

*Mum coughs. That's Mum's voice when she's on her own. Dad thinks Mum suffers from a dust allergy, but Mum doesn't think so. Mum's speech is soft and low, especially when she's telling a story. Once, my friend got Mum on the phone and thought she*

*was a man. Sometimes, Mum mumbles. That's when she's got*
*pins in her mouth.*

*That's what Mum's voice is like.*


Occasionally, some sawdust gets dislodged and falls through
the gap in the ceiling on to the pillow, because there are lots
of places where the gaps aren't covered. At night, you can
hear the sawdust shifting on its own, and things stirring,
alive. Caterpillars tick, squirrels dig, wasps scratch at paint.
In winter, frost makes the timbers tighten, and snow presses
against the door of the shed, making it stick. Spring sets off
tapping and popping on the roof; sometimes the noises go
on for several nights before anything happens. The roof pre-
pares for an attack, like an army: it moves and drips quietly.
Then, finally, comes the night when the mass of ice that has
formed on the roof works itself loose: it begins to move, a
single sheet hundreds of kilos in weight, to slide, rumbling,
down the tin roof. The chunks of ice fall past the windows
on to the ground. The din is so great that, for a moment, I
think the world is coming to an end.

The loosening of the ice is followed by silence. The house
is full of silence; the walls rise from wintry heaviness; the
shed door opens again. There are heaps of icy bodies outside.
Dad goes to hack at them with a spade.

MUM IN THE APPLE TREE. *In autumn, the three apple trees of Sawdust House fill with apples. Mum goes outside every morning with a bowl and picks up the fallen fruit. Then she asks me to stand guard while she climbs up the tree. Mum stands where a branch forks in two, and shakes. At first, she looks clumsy, but after she's been there for a bit, shaking, she gets the knack of being in the trees again. She smiles and becomes lighter, and the branches catch her power. The grass says, bump, bump when the apples thud down. I've got to watch where they fall. The tree sways and rustles, and underneath Mum there's thudding.*

*The kitchen smells of apple. Mum peels, slices, fills the dehydrator, bags apple crisps, boils jam and freezes purée.*

*Wasps buzz in the windows; they're big and sluggish. A soundless cloud of fruit flies bursts out every time you lift the lid of the compost bucket.*

In the evenings, when I'm in bed and Mum's stroking my cheek, her hands smell of apple jam.

That's what Mum's like in the apple tree.


MUM ALIVE. Mum clears the vegetable patch. She wants to get the soil warm as soon as possible. She turns the earth over with a spade and puts covers on top of it, even though Dad thinks she could just wait another two weeks. Mum's wearing a straw hat, and she waves as Dad and I go off to buy new summer tyres for the car. She stands there, leaning on the spade, hat a bit crooked, waving. She's wearing muddy gardening gloves.

That's what Mum's like alive.


That's what Mum was like when she was alive.

We eat ice creams as the tyres are being exchanged. The old tyres aren't thrown away – they're piled on to the back seat, because Mum's going to use them to build a pyramid at the edge of the garden, then fill it with earth and plant strawberries there. Because the back seat is filled with tyres, I'm allowed to sit in the front.

We drive into the front garden.

Dad picks up two of the old tyres from the back seat and starts carrying them into the garden. I follow him. We plan to wash the tyres and then help Mum fill them with earth. Mum's shown us a picture of a strawberry pyramid in a magazine.

There are five stone steps at the corner of the house.

'Look, Dad. Ice,' I say, pointing at the crushed ice on the steps.

'Can't be,' Dad replies. 'Maybe Mum's broken a glass?'

I pick up a piece. It's cold and wet, bluish.

Just then Dad reaches the top step, and a scream escapes from his mouth. The tyres drop and roll down the steps towards me. Dad looks at the garden and then at me. His eyes are huge and white; his mouth is open. When he shouts, I see teeth.

'No, Saara! Don't look!'

The first tyre hits my knee; the second rolls past me. Dad stumbles, on the tyres and me. My leg hurts, and my bottom, and my elbow.

'Don't look, Saara, don't look, don't look, Saara, nonono…'

His eyes are scaring me. I cry, but Dad doesn't comfort me, Dad roars, Dad calls for help, we fall on the steps and I'm in pain. Dad yanks me by the wrist, away, away, away, though I'm not on my feet and my arm feels like it's being ripped off.

'You mustn't look!' Dad screams. I don't know what he's talking about, but Dad screams the same thing again and again, tearing at my hand all the time.

We run, I don't know where, it goes on all day and night and the whole of the following week. 'No no no!' Dad's still shouting when the police come, people come. I don't know where we are, why Dad keeps screaming. Someone shakes him, so hard that in the end he throws up.

## I I

At school, we were told about Lot's family. The angels said to them, 'Go, but don't look back. We'll do a Bad Thing to these people. We'll rescue you, but you mustn't see what happens.' And then Lot's family started running away, but Lot's wife didn't believe the angels and looked back. And she saw the terrible Bad Thing the angels were doing to the people, and she turned into a pillar of salt. Lot's wife turned into a pillar because she couldn't bear what she saw. The teacher said the transformation was magic performed by angels, but I know now that you can freeze into a pillar without magic. It's enough that you see something you can't bear.

There are things that don't go away with time. They don't dim, soften or fade into memories. They stay as hard and as big as ever. They stand like a pillar in a person's stomach and chest and boom there. They may be forgotten, but when they come back to your mind, they are always now, and always equally big, as if they were happening right now.

The angels do Bad Things. Sometimes they give advance warning, sometimes they don't.

That day, Dad's mind received such a bad image that it will never be deleted. That image got in through Dad's eyes to his brain and destroyed a spot there. Every time something reminds him of that morning, the morning is here again. I didn't get the image because Dad pushed me away just in time. Dad said sorry for hurting my leg and bottom and elbow. Bruises heal, but images that reach the brain don't. Dad got a lump of salt inside him, and broke.

I never saw Mum again.

A week after Mum's death, I was allowed to go and see the garden with Auntie Annu and a policeman. There was a hole in the porch. Mum's garden spade had been taken away. There was a large stain on the ground, a bit like a snow angel, and a line in the soil traced by heels. It was Mum's place: the last trace of Mum, like the print of a wet bottom on a sauna bench before it evaporates.

'Well, then, how about…?' the policeman said, drawing me away. He was large and sweaty, and seemed uncomfortable.

There was no ice left. The garden looked as it did before. The ice had gone through the porch and Mum, then melted away.

Inside, in the kitchen, there were more police officers. No one said anything. None of them wanted me to ask anything.

Auntie Annu held my hand. She was carrying a bag in the other hand, with clothes for Dad and me in it. She squeezed my hand with her own, which was roughened by wool and water, and said, 'We'll be off, then.'

'We'll be in touch if there's anything else…' said the large, sweaty policeman. He had no intention of gathering us all together in the living room and revealing the truth. He wouldn't stay behind for blackcurrant juice. He didn't want to explain. He wanted to go.

The officers walked out of the front door in a line.

Auntie locked up Sawdust House.

## 12

The morning after Mum's death, Auntie Annu came to see us. We were in hospital, because Dad had been put under sedation there. A bed had been made up for me next to him.

That morning, the door opened and Auntie Annu walked in. She looked us straight in the eye, walked across the room and gave us each a long hug. She was the first person to look me in the eye after Mum's death. Her eyes were like two holes you could see in through, but she still didn't look past me.

'You're coming to the manor house,' Auntie Annu said. She started collecting our things. 'You'll stay until next week, at least.'

Dad didn't answer. He did get up and put on his shoes, though.

I started jumping, because it felt so good that someone had come to get us and had looked us in the eye.

Dad slumped back on to the bed and took me in his arms. I would have liked to comfort Dad and say something, but I couldn't. I made a tortoise out of Dad's fingers. You leave the ring finger at the bottom and bend all the other fingers over it. Then, finally, you push the thumb inside the shell. After I had folded the fingers of both hands, Auntie put our bag on her shoulder and said quietly, 'Let's go.'

Dad carried me into the car and sat next to me on the back seat. The tortoises fell apart. Dad held on to his head as if he were afraid it would come loose and fall off. The whole time, Dad kept saying, 'It doesn't make any sense. It doesn't make any sense. It doesn't make any sense.'

Auntie gave him a pill from a bottle the nurse had prescribed, and after a bit, Dad's words slowed down and he leaned his head against the window.

That's how we moved into the manor house. Auntie made some spicy soup and said we had to eat a little bit every day. After the first night, she drove to Sawdust House, packed a bag with clean clothes and toys she found in a cupboard, and wellies that were too small. She brought a board game, too, but no one wanted to play.

Auntie Annu is Dad's big sister, and she looks after Dad, even though she teased him as a child. When she was little, she cheated Dad out of chocolates and once left him on his own in the park. But she looked us in the eye and brought us home.

At school, the teacher told the class that my mother had died. Then my classmates were allowed to ask questions. I don't know what they asked, because I wasn't there. I had already heard enough questions, from the police, the nurse and Dad.

Then my classmates were allowed to draw. I saw the drawings at the spring fete. The teacher passed round handicrafts and drawings for pupils to take home, but Mum's death pictures stayed in a separate pile on her desk. They showed aeroplanes breaking into pieces in the sky, or crashing against a wall, or dropping a bomb. Someone had drawn a woman being hit on the head by a box. She had two crosses for eyes and her tongue was sticking out.

These drawings were not handed out or taken home. What could you do with drawings like that? Even my teacher couldn't find a use for them. That's why they stayed there on the desk.


Time stopped. I couldn't think forwards or backwards. Someone drew a thick white line round our thoughts, and the thoughts stopped, and we got stuck there.

Every day was its own separate day that didn't lead to anything. And every day was like the previous one. Auntie woke us up in the morning, forced us to eat three times a day and put us to bed at night. I can't remember what the food was, but it stuck in my throat and was hard to chew. My chin was tired and I chewed so hard my last milk tooth started wiggling. Dad cried into his coffee. His tears dripped on to the surface of the black liquid. Otherwise, nothing happened.

A silence fell around Dad and me. The shopkeeper lady and the PE teacher, who was on summer holiday, hugged me on a shopping trip, but no one said anything. I remember the shop lady felt soft, and she squeezed me harder than I had expected. The PE teacher looked soft, too, because she was on summer holiday and she was wearing a dress and had flowers for her balcony in her shopping basket. Well, well, the grown-ups said again, all you can do is, what can you say, yes. Let's hope time will heal. But time-heals was a pile of shit, and it was useless, anyway, because time wasn't moving, and we were stuck.

Then words ran out. All that remained were sweaty policemen and classmates clutching coloured pencils.

# 13

Mum often read fairy tales. She had a whole row of fairy-tale books on the shelf.

But the stories remained unfinished in the evening. The next day we started a new one because we had lost the bookmark or forgotten which story we were reading.

It didn't bother Mum; she wasn't interested in endings.

'The endings are always the same,' Mum said. 'The prince and princess get married and the murderer goes to prison. The interesting stuff happens before that.'

Mum also added her own elements. Sometimes she skipped over the dull bits; sometimes she went off on inventive tangents. I never spotted the exact point at which Mum moved off the page of the book – it was only afterwards I'd realize: no way is this the actual story.

'One day, a prince rode to the scene. He saw the dead maiden in the glass coffin, and his heart was filled with love for this unknown girl. The prince asked the dwarfs to open the coffin lid. "She's started to smell," the dwarfs warned him –'

'Mum! It doesn't say that.'

'The prince bent over to kiss Snow White, and indeed, the maiden's breath smelled quite foul, and the prince hesitated –'

'Mum!'

' "Shame I didn't bring a toothbrush and mouthwash for her to gargle," the prince mused.'

I said I wanted her to put the book away if she didn't feel like reading properly, and then she could make up whatever stories she wanted. But for some reason Mum preferred mashing up existing fairy tales. Maybe the pictures in the books gave her ideas. Or maybe she just liked winding me up.


When Mum died, there was a fairy tale we never got to finish. The tale went like this:

Once upon a time, there was a brother and a sister. An icy wizard came from the North. He snatched the sister and took her to his icy castle. The brother looked for his sister but instead met a wolf in the forest.

The wolf said, 'I know a man who can help you. But you'll have to pay him a golden egg.'

'Where do I find a golden egg?' the brother asked.

'Jump on my back,' the wolf answered.

The boy did so, and the wolf ran through the forest until they came to an old house.

The wolf said, 'In that chicken shed there is a hen that lays a golden egg every night.'

The brother went outside and met an old woman.

'Good day,' he said. 'May I have a golden egg from your chicken shed? I only have three coins.'

'You may,' replied the old woman, 'but keep your coins. In exchange I want a horse with a white mane.'

'Where do I find a horse with a white mane?' the brother asked the wolf.

The wolf replied, 'Jump on my back.'

And so the brother jumped on the wolf's back and the wolf rode through the forest till they came to a riverbank. On the other side of the river was a herd of horses in a pasture. One of the horses had a white mane.

The brother walked over to a youth who was sitting on a stone.

'May I have that horse with the white mane?' he asked the youth. 'I have three coins.'

'You may,' replied the youth, 'but keep your coins. In exchange I want a silver bird.'

'Where do I find a silver bird?' the brother asked sadly upon returning to the wolf.

The wolf said, 'Jump on my back.'

And so the brother jumped on the wolf's back, and the wolf ran along the riverbank till they came to the seashore. A large sailing ship was floating in the harbour.

'The captain of that ship has a silver bird,' the wolf said.

The brother walked to the ship. 'May I have a silver bird?' the brother asked. 'I've only got three coins.'

The captain laughed at the boy's money. 'You can buy a silver bird all right, but by way of payment, I want a rope that will never break.'

And again the brother went back to the wolf.

'Where do I find such a rope?'

'Jump on my back,' the wolf said.

And so the brother jumped on the wolf's back again, and the wolf ran along the coast to the next town, and then the next one, and there it stopped in front of a red-brick factory.

'They make eternal ropes in this factory,' the wolf said.

The brother went inside the factory and saw that it was just one enormous, long hall with ropes of differing thickness running from one end to the other. Huge winches twisted the ropes, under the surveillance of a fox dressed in trousers and a waistcoat.

The brother went up to the fox.

'I'd like to buy an eternal rope. But I've only got three coins.'

'That could work. But in return I want a stone that has been brought down from the moon,' the fox replied.

And so on. I'm not sure at what point I realized Mum's story was going round in a circle, but I went on listening for a bit even after the rope factory – the stone that came from the moon belonged to a professor who wanted the world's wisest book in payment; the book was found in the attic of a librarian, who in payment wanted a blue jewel, which was found at a baker's. The baker wanted llama's milk in payment – but then both Mum and I got fed up, and I said, 'Let's stop now.'

And Mum replied, 'Next instalment tomorrow.'

'I don't want to hear you telling all that backwards,' I sighed.

'Let's invent another ending. The sister can stay in the icy castle. Let's organize a world rally championship for the brother.'

'No way.'

'I'll think of something.'

And perhaps Mum did. Perhaps the ending to the fairy tale was just what Mum had stopped to think about in the garden when her head split open.


My last two images of Mum: the bedtime story the previous night, and leaving the garden the next morning. Mum in her sun hat, wearing gardening gloves. It's as if the two moments were lit up with a special, radiant light.

A spring evening on the sofa, a spring morning, and the buzzing of flies.

# 14

'Why? Why? Why Hannele?' Dad moans at night in Auntie's kitchen, holding his head. 'Where the hell is the sense?'

I lie in bed, trying not to hear. But the sound carries through the stove, which connects directly to the kitchen through the flue, and I can't escape it. The small black stove in the corner wails, pressed against the wall of my room, its flue about to choke. What a terribly sad little stove, I think.

Why, why, why.

Dad has so many questions that no one wants to listen to. I still listen, a little bit. Perhaps Auntie can answer one of the questions, at least; she is a big sister after all. I could have become a big sister if there had been other babies. But only I came out when Mum's stomach was cut open, so now I'm no one's sister – I'm just myself.

'It could have been anyone,' Auntie answers. 'Anyone could have been outside at that moment. A lot of people *were* outside then.'

'I want to be angry with someone!' the stove howls.

When Dad howls, his voice comes from the pit of his stomach. Dad's back bends and he starts shaking in time with his crying. Dad cries like a small child: he oozes snot and spit and wipes his eyes with his big grown-up's fists like a giant. I'm afraid that Dad will get cramp or hiccups or have a heart attack. His clothes will tear, the seams will squeal, Dad will fall apart.

When Dad cries, I concentrate on looking at Auntie Annu. I think: 'If Auntie starts howling now, too, I'll explode. I'll fall apart with all this wailing. I'll become a pile of bread-crumbs, jumping about from the crying. The tips of my fingers, my hair and my knees will tremble with the crying of the grown-ups.'

But Auntie doesn't howl. She doesn't fall apart or tremble or burst into tears. Not once. Not even inside the stove in the evenings when I should be asleep.

Auntie does cry. She sheds tears without always noticing it herself. She cries many times a day. Auntie cooks and heats up stoves. She dashes to Sawdust House, to the shop, to the undertaker's and back in the car. She holds me on her lap and dresses me in woolly jumpers. And above all, Auntie felts wool in her workshop. She rubs, thumps, throws around and rolls up large pieces of wool. Water and soap splash, stuff becomes felt, it shrinks, tightens and strengthens. Auntie's tears fly.

But she's still in one piece.


'Wool helps,' Auntie Annu assures us.

She dresses us in woollen jumpers and woollen socks. She makes our beds with sheepskins and woollen blankets. We even have cushions covered in sheepskin. Auntie believes that the sadder a person, the warmer they must be kept. And Dad and I are really sad. Our foreheads drip with sweat as Auntie heats stoves, makes soup seasoned with chilli and takes care we don't remove our woollen jumpers.

'Wool breathes. It keeps you warm even when it's wet; airing makes it clean; it doesn't smell; it heals wounds, ear infections and athlete's foot. Just think of Inuit babies! They're wrapped in wool and kept in those swaddling clothes with their wee and poo for a whole month. You can't go changing nappies in that sort of cold. And when the swaddling clothes are cut open a month later, they're not even dirty. That's the wonder of wool!'


'Was there something I could have done?' Dad goes on in the stove, after a while, in a smaller voice.

'No,' Auntie Annu answers.

'If I had been in the garden then, I might just have got there in time. Say if I had pushed Hannele...'

'You couldn't have.'

Auntie Annu's replies thud, as wet wool does when she throws it on the floor. Despite the wool and Auntie Annu, Dad goes on and on, night after night. He creaks and drips like an icy mass on a tin roof, until he starts to fear the loosening of his feet and hands.

Dad claims there's something wrong with his nerves, because sometimes he can't feel anything in his feet or hands.

'I'm getting brittle,' Dad splutters, squeezing his toes.

Dad's broken. It happens so easily. Mum's image has got to Dad's brain, and now the only sound it makes is why why why. Dad's got a hole in his head and a lump of salt in his chest, and now he's getting brittle. I didn't know that could happen to a living creature.


Sometimes, ice is so cold it burns your hands.

And sometimes, when you go from a hot sauna into ice-cold water, and then you get out of the water, the cold air feels warm. And sometimes, when your fingers are cold from being outside, and you put them under a lukewarm tap, the water feels scalding.

'I feel nothing!' Dad says.

Perhaps he's got hot and cold mixed up.

## 15

For Easter, we went to church with school. It was called a children's service, and Matti and Leila, the ministers, and Niina, from the youth group, acted the parts of the disciples and the women at Jesus' tomb. I know Easter is because Jesus died on the cross but for some reason, they tried to avoid talking about that in the children's service.

I was already interested in the crucifixion, because I had never really understood it. I waited for the play to get to the part about Jesus' arrest. Leila the minister and Niina from the youth group were grieving disciples. But then all that happened was that we were told there was a thunderclap, a curtain was torn and darkness fell. In the next scene it was morning, Jesus' tomb was empty and everyone was happy.

I wanted someone to explain how you can die of nails going through your hands and feet. Sometimes a whole hand or foot can work itself loose and the person still doesn't die.

But maybe grown-ups don't like talking about death, even though they're going to die themselves. When you eat, you grow, and when you become an adult, you die.

Sometimes a person dies easily; sometimes the hard way. Mum and Jesus died easily: Mum in the middle of ordinary gardening jobs, and Jesus from four nails. Those are the sorts of deaths grown-ups don't want to talk about.

What Matti the minister was able to explain was why they wanted to kill Jesus. They wanted to stop him from getting more disciples. When Jesus spoke, he grew and slithered like wires inside a wall, and they didn't like it. And so they stopped Jesus by nailing him to a cross. That's how Easter came about. That's why everything grows at Easter. The minister dresses in green, and you plant ryegrass in yogurt pots, even though Jesus just died. People eat yogurt and their bones and muscles grow, and in the picture on the milk carton, a strong girl carries her little brother.

On Easter morning, I said to Mum and Dad that I didn't want to eat, because then you grow up and die. Mum said, 'You'll grow in any case. But if you don't eat, you'll become an angry grown-up.'

I was annoyed, though. Why hadn't anybody drawn death on the side of the milk carton?

# 16

It was nice hearing Auntie Annu talking about the manor house.

'When I moved to Extra Great Manor, I didn't do anything at first. I walked slowly from one room to another; I took my time looking at each room. I looked out of every window, I walked round the garden. "Who are you?" That's what I asked this house. Then I started cleaning. I cleaned every room, but I didn't throw anything out. I listened to the doors creaking and the walls popping, and I practised heating the wood stove in a way that would stop it letting in smoke. Then one day, I had cleaned everything and the manor house started talking.'

'What did it say?' I asked.

'It said, "Go ahead, set up a workshop." And I asked where the best place would be. And Manor House replied, "The guest stable. You may set it up there." '

Auntie's workshop has a tiled floor and a shower, like in a swimming pool, and metal vats big enough for me to have a bath in, if I wanted. It smells of wet wool and soap. Auntie's wool products are big and thick and they're hung on the walls.

Today, Auntie is about to start a new piece. I watch her spreading the base material on the giant table in the middle of the workshop. The table is so large that when there's a celebration in the manor house, all the guests can fit round it. At least twenty candles burn in a candelabra that stands in the middle of the table.

But the candelabra isn't there now, the table is clean, and Auntie spreads the thick, flame-red fabric over its surface. She takes off her socks, rolls up her trouser legs and picks up a bucket. Then she dissolves some Marseille soap in a bucket of water and stirs it with her hand while looking at the blank red fabric. The soapy water is hot, and Auntie's hand goes red, too.

Auntie has already selected wisps of wool in different colours and placed them in a wheelbarrow. Now she climbs on to the table and starts arranging the wool on top of the base. First she creates the foundation, then on top of that she lays thinner strands in different colours. Auntie crawls around the colourful cloud that rises from the surface of the table, every now and then standing up to get a better view.

'Is it fire?' I ask, because I see red, yellow and orange, and it's a bit boring just watching her prepare the table.

'No,' Auntie Annu says, not looking at me.

'It looks like fire to me,' I say, but Auntie's not listening any more.

At last, the felting process begins. Auntie wets the whole piece of fabric and the patterns on it with soapy water. Then she climbs onto the fabric on her hands and knees, and starts making circling motions with her fingers. Eventually, her whole palm gets involved. Auntie adds soapy water and the fabric bubbles under her fingers. That's how the patterns stick to the fabric. Next, Auntie wraps the fabric inside a bamboo curtain and starts rolling it back and forth on the floor. It's a bit like she's making a gigantic red sushi roll. Water and lather drizzle onto the floor through the bamboo sticks, and Auntie Annu crawls among the mess. Every now and then, she opens the roll, checks what the fabric looks like, fixes a strip that's come loose and carries on rolling. The big, soft wisps have now become thin stripes, and the woollen clouds have turned into lumpy patches.

At last, the rolling stops. Auntie opens the bamboo curtain and takes out the fabric. It has shrunk and become patterned. Auntie spreads the fabric over the table, stands up and assesses it.

'It needs more...' Auntie mutters, going to get more wisps. She arranges more colours in a couple of places, rubs them with her finger to make them stick, stands up again, looks.

Then Auntie takes off her shirt and trousers. She looks at me as if she's just remembered I'm in the room with her. She's wearing a black bra. A small tattooed lizard's head peeks out from under the edge. When I was little, I always wanted to open Auntie's shirt buttons and tickle the lizard.

'There's going to be some splashing,' Auntie Annu warns.

I'm not worried. This is the best bit about felting.

Auntie pours more soapy water out of the bucket, grabs a corner of the fabric and starts thumping and throwing it along the tiled floor. She lifts the wet fabric and smacks it down, again and again. The soapy water flies all over the walls, and even my face gets wet. The thumping is called 'frightening the fibres'. When the fibres get frightened, they become fluffy and matted. That way, the fabric tightens and becomes thick.

Lifting a large piece of wet woollen fabric is hard work. Auntie sweats, dances round the room with the fabric, water splashing.

I dry my face on my sleeve and go to explore the store-room. It's next to the workshop and it's where Auntie keeps her wool. There are rolls of fabric and balls of yarn of different sizes. The felting wool comes in balls that look like candyfloss – Auntie keeps these in transparent plastic drawers on a set of shelves that covers the whole of one wall. The wool wisps come in all colours: bright red, yellow and turquoise, lots of different shades of blue and green, oranges, purples, browns, greys and blacks. Some of the wools are rough; others are straight and smooth like angel's hair. If you touch them for long enough, your hands get all greasy.

Apart from wool, the storeroom houses glass jars with all sorts of small objects in them. Auntie uses them to decorate felted things after they've dried and shrunk to the right size. There are silver threads, dried leaves, beads and coins, cinnamon sticks, smooth driftwood, rusty nails, old photos, buttons, fraying zips, dried beans: almost anything you can attach to fabric with a needle.

I look at the wools and finger the whitest one. It's soft and fine, as if someone had brushed it straight after sauna. There are so many different shades of white next to it that I get confused: I don't understand what white actually is any more. There are so many whites between grey, yellow and brown. But when does grey become white? When does white become yellow?

Everything is difficult. There is no boundary between the colours: white is yellow, and Bruno's brown is black. Cold burns, and frosty air warms. Dad's toes exist, but they disappear.

# 17

Halfway through June, Auntie Annu goes to Sawdust House to get us summer clothes. Dad and I don't go with her. Dad doesn't go because he still doesn't want to visit the house. I don't go because I don't want to leave Dad on his own.

Auntie comes back bringing two bags of stuff. I get sandals, a summer jacket, two dresses – one of them doesn't fit me any more – shirts, a thinner nightdress and a tracksuit. Dad gets shorts, sandals and ordinary clothes. He's already got sunglasses. The other bag holds a swimsuit and swimming trunks, my sun hat and Dad's cap.

There's a pile of post at the bottom of the bag. Dad goes through the letters. He puts the ones for Mum on one side, only opening his own.

'I can take care of those if you like,' Auntie Annu says, pointing at Mum's letters.

'They're just junk mail,' Dad says, waving his hand.

'Still, they can be notified.'

'I suppose so.'

Auntie picks up the bundle. She doesn't say anything else.

'I think I'll take a look at the woodshed door,' Dad mutters. He puts his sunglasses on, and goes out.

'Why do you smell of grass?' I ask Auntie.

'I mowed your lawn,' Auntie replies. 'It was a jungle, the whole garden.'

'When are we going back home?'

'I don't know,' Auntie replies. She thinks of adding something, I can tell, but decides not to.

I put on the sun hat. I think of Sawdust House, standing in the middle of a jungle, and of the living-room wall, my picture smiling under its panelling. The picture stands and waits, frozen there as it was one renovation day two years ago. It wears a stripy top and turquoise tights, and has its back against the sooty wallpaper, with the wooden panel of the living room acting as its cover. And no one's told her we've left. And no one knows when we're coming back.

I go into the sheep enclosure. Bruno runs up to me and says baa. He still follows me even though I don't give him milk from a bottle any more. I tickle him above his tail, which makes it twitch and look really funny and silly.

Sheep always want to be as high up as possible. The lambs climb on to their mums' backs and stand there, and the grown-up ones are always fighting over a place on the roof of Dad's car. They'll climb into the fountain and jump on to tree stumps and wooden blocks and the wheelbarrow.

'Sheep are quite thick,' Auntie Annu has to admit.

That evening, I lie in my hospital bed in the summer nightie Auntie fetched for me. When I turn over, the lowered side rails clatter. One of the wheel locks below is broken, causing the bed to move.

I look at the walls around me. I draw a line around them, and my room stays inside the line. Apart from the secret room, that is: my room is now the one with the panel that clicks to open a door into another space. I stop drawing to wonder whether the secret room belongs to my room or the one next door. Or does the secret room belong to itself? Or doesn't it have a line at all, because it's secret? Are secrets precisely the sort of thing that remain outside lines? Is that the way detectives solve murder mysteries, by seeing the gaps that secrets leave in the lines?

Sometimes too many thoughts crowd into my head. That makes the grey cells boil; it's like everything's about to burst out of my brain. That's when I call my favourite Belgian detective for help. He takes a chalk and draws a white outline. When my thoughts are inside the line, they settle down. He knows the number of guests has to be right – not too many and not too few. The thoughts have to fit into one room. And if some thought or object is of no use, then out it goes.

# 18

Dad spends the whole of June in bed wearing sunglasses. He bangs his foot against the bars of the hospital bed – bang, bang, bang – so that even my room vibrates. When I peer in from the door and ask what the matter is, Dad replies, 'I can't feel my toes!'

And bang, the metal clatters again.

'What's happening to my feet?' Dad asks. He stares at me as if he doesn't know I'm his little girl.

I take the quilt off Dad's feet and have a look.

'There's nothing there,' I say.

'What? They're not there?' Dad's all worked up now. He presses his hands against his face, starts rubbing: his whole forehead moves up and down, as if the skin on his face were loose.

'Can't you see my toes?' he asks through the gaps between his fingers.

'No, I mean they look normal.'

'What?'

'Your feet look normal.'

'Can you pinch them?' Dad asks.

Dad's toes are ugly and lumpy, with hair here and there, and I don't really want to touch them. The skin underneath is thick. It peels off in dry, white strips. The nails are yellow, especially on his big toes.

I pinch them anyway. I hold one toe at a time between my thumb and index finger and squeeze. I start with the left big toe and carry on to the smaller ones, then I do the same with the right foot. Finally, I do rain going pitter-patter on Dad's soles and he calms down.

'Thank you, Saara,' Dad says, pulling his feet under the quilt.


Bang, bang, bang: the same knocking against the wall.

'My toes! Somebody do something!' Dad shouts in his room.

This time Dad's sitting up. He's curled up on the edge of the bed, knees tucked under his chin, holding his toes.

'They're falling off,' Dad says. 'Have I caught a cold or what?'

'What do you mean?' I ask.

'My toes are falling off,' Dad answers.

'Can I have a look?'

Dad shakes his head, clutching his toes more tightly. There's nothing unusual-looking about his feet: no bleeding, at least.

'Shall I pinch them?' I ask, though really, I just want to go away.

Dad shakes his head.

'I'm going,' I say, and I head back to my own room.

Then Auntie Annu comes upstairs.

'Come on, Pekka, now, really…' she mutters, going into Dad's room.

I'm in the middle of drawing something. I put my palm on a piece of paper and draw round it with a pen. I've got five fingers. The little finger is a bit apart from the others; the index finger is slightly crooked. I swap hands. A familiar hand. Once, at school, everyone was allowed to draw their hands on a big wall, and even though there were two hundred hands on the wall, I recognized my own straight away. That's how familiar they were.

'Stroke me!' Dad shouts behind the wall, because Auntie Annu has already gone back downstairs.

I don't really want to go. I pretend I'm the lord of the castle who has trapped a maiden inside a wall.

*Once upon a time, there was a maiden who lived in a castle and who fell in love with the wrong knight. This was judged to be punishable.*

I thought of a suitable punishment for the maiden.

The maiden shouts: 'Help! Somebody stroke me!'

*But the maiden was carried into the castle courtyard where a new wall was being built. The maiden was placed inside the wall. The whole time the stones were being laid, the maiden shouted and screamed, but in the end she was fully covered by the stones and her voice fell silent.*

*This was a familiar business to the lord of the castle. He had confined naughty maidens many times before, and he didn't care one little bit about the maiden's cries, or her toes.*

*Even the next day, moaning could be heard from inside the wall. On the third day, the moaning stopped. Three years went by, and a birch tree grew on the spot where the maiden had been buried.*

In the evening, Dad comes downstairs. He sits at the table and strokes the wall, deep in thought. The bowl of fish stew Auntie Annu made sits in front of him, getting cold.

'This sort of surface, you never know what's inside it at the end of the day.'

'I can tell you it's timber,' Auntie answers.

'Yes, but what condition is it in? You never –'

'Yes, yes,' Auntie Annu says, tired of Dad's talk.

But Dad presses on: 'You never know. You see a wall, and it looks like a wall: it's got wallpaper and skirting boards, and everything is as it should be. Just as it should be. Then one day, you decide to replace the wallpaper with wood panelling. So you tear off the chipboard and realize something is crumbling there at the back. You hit a log with the hammer and feel it sinking. You dig into the timber with your fingers; your whole hand goes through the wall. What was meant to last is rotten. I've heard these stories. Then people ask: did you really not know? How come you didn't notice? Didn't you have any inkling at all?'

'This house is a healthy old house, whatever you say,' Auntie repeats.

Dad looks out of the window. The sheep are eating grass. The sun is shining.

'Then you realize that the whole house stayed standing because it was propped up by the wrong things: door frames, window frames. There were no supporting structures, just brittle stuff, and the weather was calm enough for the wind not to blow the house down. An ordinary day, chipboard, a morning in the garden. Then suddenly things fall from the sky and your hand sinks into the wall.'

And having said that, Dad presses his head against the backing paper.


Mum used to stroke Dad's back. Mum used to say what Dad was like.

'You need a haircut,' she would say. 'You look tired. You look handsome. It doesn't suit you. It suits you. Why are you asking me when you've clearly made up your mind! You *can* do it. We're here now, now we're here.'

Perhaps Mum always said what Dad was like, where Dad ended and the rest began, but now that Mum's dead, Dad is brittle. His outline's leaky, the white line's blurred, his feet disappear.

I'd like to say: 'Lean against the wall, Dad; I'll draw your line.'

Then Dad could look at the picture, and colour it in with felt tips. And then he'd see what a big man he really is.

# 19

Sometimes, aeroplanes spring leaks, say in a water pipe or the toilet. That's a fact. If the water that drips out is blue, it's from the toilet; if it's clear, it comes from somewhere else. If the aeroplane is stationary, the drops of water will just fall straight down to the ground. Up in the air, the seeping water will freeze because of the low temperature outside.

A lump of ice that forms during a long flight can be as big as a football. When the aeroplane loses altitude and the air temperature rises, the chunk of ice might detach itself from the aeroplane and drop down on to the ground. Ice is the most common thing to fall from an aeroplane. And when, underneath, there is somebody's garden, where a person in the middle of planning a strawberry pyramid is doing jobs, that individual might be hit on the head with a lump of ice the size of a football and die. That is a fact.

Dad has started sitting in front of the computer. He looks normal again – perhaps because he has swapped the sunglasses for spectacles and put on his day clothes. Or because his toes aren't leaking any more. But now he sits in front of the computer, reading and clicking and not listening properly. Auntie Annu tries to get him to do some work, because the sheep enclosure has got to be moved and the composting container emptied, but Dad just growls.

'Oh, well, that's how it is. Listen to this,' Dad begins again.

I'd like to slip away, upstairs.

'There's this list here. This just beggars belief. How come it's not talked about more? Engines. In August 2000, one of the engines of a KLM aeroplane fell out. The captain managed an emergency landing on a beach. Doors. In March 2005, a door fell off a British Airways Boeing 747 and the plane had to make an emergency landing. The door missed a couple out on a walk by just twenty metres. Tyre. In May 2001, the right-hand tyre of a Blue Panorama Airlines plane fell off. Mount. In October 1999, a tyre mount worked itself loose from a Delta Airlines plane and fell into the middle of a quiet suburb.'

Dad pauses and looks at me and Auntie Annu expectantly. It's good that Dad's finally doing something and that he's put on his day clothes, but I think he's overdoing this computer thing.

'And there's more: meteorites. On 30 November 1954, Ann Elisabeth Hodges was having a nap in her living room when a four-kilo meteorite fell through her roof, bounced off the radio and hit her on the hip.'

Dad shows us an image of Hodges he's found on the internet. Ann has a really big bruise on her hip.

'Fish. When a warm air mass meets a cold one, this can create small tornadoes which suck fish and other sea life out of the water and transport them to dry land. Toads. In 1794, hundreds of toads with tails rained on French soldiers. Golf balls. In 1969, hundreds of golf balls rained down in Florida. Though it does say here that there are cases where the tornado theory doesn't really work. In northern Greece, the only thing that came down was anchovies.'

'Perhaps an aeroplane dropped its cargo,' Auntie Annu suggests.

'But in 1859, in Wales, it only rained sticklebacks. In those days aeroplanes didn't even exist!' Dad looks at us over his glasses, as if waiting for a solution. 'Besides, the stickleback isn't a shoal fish, so no tornado could have filtered out sticklebacks and left other fish in the water, never mind stones and clumps of seaweed. Did you know about all this?' Dad asks Auntie Annu. 'When you look at these dates, almost every year in some part of the world, some door or engine or whatever falls off. I mean, if a couple of stones hit some windows on houses near a building site, it makes the news and the company gets taken to court. But think about it, what if a whole jet engine falls on the roof?'

'I imagine that would be on the evening news,' Auntie says.

'Well, I never got to hear about it!'

'Didn't happen in Finland.'

And Dad's list goes on.

'Money. In 1940, it rained old rouble coins in the Soviet Union. Scientists believe that erosion had gradually exposed a treasure trove of coins. The wind had seized the treasure and rained it down.

'In 1875, on two September evenings, large crystals of sugar came down. There was no explanation for the phenomenon. In addition, spiders, starlings, worms and jelly have also descended from the sky.'

Dad stops reading and looks at us again.

'Jelly?' Auntie Annu says.

'Yep. Spiders, starlings, worms and jelly. There's no proper explanation for those last few things.'

I feel like laughing. I know I shouldn't, but I can't help it. I imagine what Mum would have looked like if it had been jelly that fell on her. Can you die of jelly? At least it sounds softer than a lump of ice the size of a football. I feel like laughing because I think Mum herself could have invented death by jelly. *Aargh-blub-blub-blub*: that's how her jelly death rattle would have sounded. Unlucky Mum, inside the jelly, would have fallen silent, but the surface of the jelly would have kept on quivering.

'Bloody hell, this is so hard,' Auntie Annu says, and suddenly starts giggling.

Dad glances at Auntie, surprised, but then snorts himself. 'What else can you say?'

And that's when Dad laughs for the first time that summer.

We laugh together: at people, dying of jelly; at stickle-backs, whirling in the sky; at couples out walking by the sea, surprised by a falling door. At angels doing Bad Things without warning.

## 20

Oh, I've seen the way Dad glances at the sky sometimes. As if he's checking something. He goes out of the door in the direction of the car, but after a couple of steps, he looks up. Just for a short while. Then he carries on. And sometimes, when the sun is behind the clouds and the light changes, he looks up to see what's going on in the sky. But it's just cloud.

As if he had only just now realized that above the garden there is always an empty sky. And beyond the sky, space, and in space, spaceships that can break.

The sky is an idea I can't draw a line round. The sky is always open. It leaks, like Dad's toes.

## 21

'Hey, Dad! Come and have a look!' I cry.

My feet are up against the trunk of the linden tree in the garden. My head is packed with blood, but I want to stay upside down until Dad sees me.

It's surprisingly hard to do a handstand and shout at the same time.

Dad's beard becomes hair, his hair becomes beard, and his ears spin on the spot. The wrong way round, Dad looks lighter, as if he had risen up into the air just a tiny bit. The sunglasses become funny, black cheeks.

'Dad, the wrinkles on your forehead are a mouth!'

I want to laugh. Suddenly, I collapse. I hear a crack and my shoulder hurts badly. 'Aaaaah!' The crack came from my shoulder.

Dad's feet are back on the ground. He runs to me and tries to lift me up. But that really hurts!

'What happened? Saara, what happened?'

I can't sit up. I've collapsed like a clothes horse. I've gone crooked; I don't know how to unfold myself. My fingers move, but otherwise I'm in a totally bizarre position.

'Saara, Saara, Saara...' Dad's panting.

'Help, Dad! It hurts!'

Dad manages to turn me round so I'm on my knees and then, slowly, so I'm in a sitting position. I didn't know you needed a shoulder to sit up. My feet are stuck because my shoulder's poking out.

'How come it's there? Why did you do that? You should never...You should have asked me to prop you up...' Dad mutters, pressing my shoulder.

'Aaaaah!'

The cry sounds so strange that Auntie comes outside, too. She looks at Dad first, and only then at me, a flattened clothes horse. Dad is small and helpless on his knees by my side. Once again, he failed to protect us from danger. I feel my shoulder with my right hand, and, yes, it's poking out in a strange direction. The world swung my shoulder out of its hole, and Dad couldn't do a thing about it.


'Hello, Saara,' the doctor says.

We've driven to the hospital, emergency lights flashing. The doctor is a hairy man. Apart from curly hair on his head, he's got stubble and hair on his neck and hands. But he has kind eyes and even though he's touching my shoulder, it doesn't hurt.

'So you were learning to do handstands,' the hairy doctor says.

'Yes, against a tree.'

'How far did you count?'

'Thirty-seven.'

Then the doctor switches on the wall-cabinet light and shows me the X-ray.

'Here's your shoulder,' the doctor begins. 'This ball should be in that hole, where it goes round. But now it's popped out, see?'

'I didn't know there was a ball like that,' I say, taking a closer look at the picture. Everything has its place, even under the skin. I think of my shoulder, then of my elbows, fingers, knees, thighs, toes and the point where the head joins the skeleton. Was it really the case that any one of them could pop out of its place at any time, if your gait's a bit off, that you could just collapse like a clothes horse? I never realized a human being was so fragile.

It's lucky I'm covered by skin! What would hold all the hands, fingers and other things together otherwise? They could just break and fall out. Without skin, everything could disintegrate. A broken arm, stomach, even the heart or liver!

'So, Saara,' the hairy doctor says, taking hold of my arm. 'Now, I've got an important question. Tell me your favourite thought.'

Every now and then, you meet grown-ups who take children seriously. They ask interesting questions and listen to your answers. You can be straight with grown-ups like that. You can ask them things and they give proper answers, and they also tell you if they don't know. I decide to test this doctor.

'I like to think about time,' I answer.

Just then, the doctor yanks my arm with terrible force. My shoulder lets out a cracking sound and my mouth lets out a cry. The doctor looks on with his calm eyes.

'Time? That's a splendid answer. Try and twist your hand now.'

'Saara? Saara?' Dad's shouting behind the door, rattling the door handle.

'It's OK, it's OK,' I tell him.

The rattling stops.

My shoulder moves normally in its socket. The pain has gone, too. I wonder for a moment if I should be angry, or thump the doctor on the nose, but this time thing interests me enough for me to decide to let it go.

'What is it about time that you find particularly interesting?' the doctor asks.

I wait for a moment, to see if he's planning to grab anything again, but as he's not touching me, I decide it's a genuine question.

'That time moves backwards, like this.' I show him with my arm, which is now back in its place. 'Here is now, and here are the things that happened a long time ago. And it moves like this.'

The doctor nods his curly head.

'But sometimes, pieces come loose and they don't move with time but instead stay here, always,' I go on. 'Everything else moves backwards, but those pieces stay here. You can forget them, but when you remember them again, they're just as close as they were at the beginning.'

'Right,' the doctor says.

'Have you got pieces like that?' I ask.

'Of course,' the doctor replies.

I wait, and he goes: 'One could be when I first held my daughter.'

'Any others?'

'Another one could be when my son started cycling without stabilizers, and I let go.'

I try to imagine the hairy doctor letting go of the bike and watching the boy cycling off. Then I say, 'I've got pieces of my mum. They're clear but they're loose.'

'I don't think it matters,' the doctor says.

'Really?'

'I think you can let the pieces be as they are.'

'OK,' I answer. 'I've also got a medical question. It's about blood.'

'Let's hear it,' the hairy doctor says.

'Why does blood look blue through the skin but red when it comes out?'

'That's a very good question! Blood running through systemic veins *is* blue as long as it remains inside the vein.

When it flows out and gets oxygenated, it becomes red. And in the same way, the heart makes the blood red because it adds oxygen to the blood.'

'Wow,' I answer. 'I've got another one: can an eye pop out of its socket if you don't blink often enough?'

The doctor looks at me, and, perhaps because of my question, blinks his dark eyes several times.

'Not really. But I specialize in X-rays – I'm not an eye expert.'

'There are no bones in the eye,' I say, nodding.

'Exactly,' the doctor replies.

'What if you sneeze hard? Can the eye come out then?'

'You can't sneeze with your eyes open,' the doctor answers.

'I know! I've tried.'

I show the doctor how I've tried to use my finger to make my eyes stay open.

'And did it work?'

'It didn't,' I answer.

The doctor winks at me.

Before I go, the doctor gives me the X-ray to take home. My popped-out shoulder glows there, blue and clear.

'You could frame it,' the hairy doctor says.

In the manor house, Auntie Annu puts the image in a golden frame, and I hang it up in my room. Not many girls have a picture showing their own skeleton.

## 22

In Sawdust House, Dad was always afraid that there was water running inside the walls. Or that there was a hole in the roof, or the drains were blocked, or a water pipe would burst. So many things could go wrong in a wooden house, and Dad had to worry about all of them.

Sometimes, when it was raining hard, Dad stood next to the wardrobe and stroked the wall.

'Do you think this is damp?' Dad asked Mum. 'Why is this so cold?'

Dad had this constant feeling that a problem would creep in stealthily – through the roof, through cracks in the walls, through the flue of the fireplace or the vents in the cellar. He felt he should spot it but might miss it, and then it'd all be too late and Sawdust House would be rotten. Or we would contract cancer from exposure to radon. Or a flue would catch fire. Or water would drip in through the roof, through the holes where nails had been hammered in, which had become enlarged, and the decayed roof would collapse on us. Or carbon monoxide would come in through loose tiles on the stove and poison us. And it would all be Dad's fault.

'Chipboard is dangerous,' Dad explained to Mum and me. 'It emits formaldehyde. We should tear open all these walls and go over to plasterboard. It would be safer from the fire-safety point of view; chipboard houses like these go up like torches. But it costs money to replace all the walls with new ones. While we're at it, we'd have to dismantle all the kitchen cabinets, and the bathroom. Chipboard's the worst possible option; God knows what kind of fungi might be breeding there…'

'Pekka, for two years we've had smoke alarms waiting in the cleaning cupboard for someone to fix them to the ceiling. Let's not get stressed about chipboard right now,' Mum said. She stroked Dad's neck.

When Mum stroked him like that, Dad growled for a bit like an unhappy dog, but settled down in the end.

'The sound of the alarms is so infuriating,' Dad muttered.

'I couldn't agree more,' Mum replied.


In the manor house, it doesn't matter if it rains hard. Dad and I sit by the window and stare at the grey, rushing curtain. Just when it seems it couldn't rain any harder, the rain falls more heavily still. I feel cosy and damp. The grey curtain rushes, the drainpipe gurgles, the roof booms and the odd drip-drip sounds from the stove as water trickles in through the chimney. There's frost and lichen between the windowpanes, and the guttering on the roof is overflowing. Raindrops beat the ground and splatter mud, and in no time at all, a large puddle forms on the sandy road.

But Dad's not worried. This chimney isn't Dad's, and Dad doesn't say, 'I should install chimney caps. This damp will make the whole chimney crumble, and where's the money to repair it?'

This is not our roof. These walls are not filled with saw-dust. There's no cellar under the house for water to run into. Nothing's mouldy. Or rather, everything's already damp and mouldy anyway.

Dad tried to protect us, but in the end, it wasn't enough. He thought too much about the walls and forgot the sky.

Now Dad just listens to the drip-drip-drip in the flue.

## 23

After a fortnight of rain, Auntie Annu suggests we go and clean the guttering of Sawdust House. Dad growls and snaps at us: he wants to take a look at the wonky ceiling in Auntie's barn.

'You could sell the place,' Auntie Annu says. 'But it's not a good idea to just leave it lying empty. It'll go to rack and ruin.'

'I was thinking of starting to dismantle that ceiling today,' Dad grunts.

Auntie Annu stares at him wordlessly.

'It wouldn't be a big deal, fixing it. Then you could use the garage side, too. At the moment there's always the worry that a beam or a plank will fall on the car.'

'It's a wooden house – it needs to be lived in,' Auntie Annu says. 'Otherwise it'll start getting damp – you know that as well as I do.'

'No,' says Dad.

'You can live in the manor house, no problem.'

'We're not going to stay here for good.'

'Can't we just go and clean the guttering?'

'I don't want to go there. For God's sake, is it so hard to grasp?' Dad suddenly starts to shout at the top of his voice. Even Auntie Annu is startled. 'I don't want to see that house, I don't want to see that garden. I can't look at the garden, because I can still picture my wife there without her head, OK? What is so hard to understand about that? What? *What is so hard?*'

One, two, three.

Time passes; Mum moves backwards.

The clock on the manor-house wall.

Mum's head. Mum without a head.

*What is so hard?*

My thoughts lose their grip. I can't stop them; they start fizzing like a peppermint when you drop it in Coca-Cola. We did that experiment with Dad once, and all the Coke fizzed out of the bottle. Dad protected me and dropped a tyre on me.

I slide out of my chair and slip upstairs. I bet Dad will start falling apart and trembling again, and soon the stove will howl. I worry that someone will come after me; I don't want anyone right now. So I go and hide in the library. I shut the door and jump up on to the windowsill and sit down behind the curtains.

Outside, it rains and rains and rains. I press my forehead against the window and close my eyes. I keep drawing a white line, round and round.

There are no books left in the library at the manor house. An old wooden desk stands in front of the window. Three armchairs and a sofa form a circle in the middle of the room. Gentlemen can sit in them, reading newspapers and smoking. There are overflowing ashtrays on both the coffee table and the desk. I get a whiff of tobacco from the windowsill. The thick velvet curtains have been absorbing it for years.

If a murder were ever committed at Extra Great Manor, this is the room where the detective would invite the guests to take a seat, as he always does at the end of the episode.

'Calm down, *mademoiselle*, there is no need to worry,' he says, drawing the velvet curtain aside. He pats my hand and points at one of the armchairs.

I shake my head and back into the corner of the windowsill.

'Mum hasn't got a head!' I cry.

'*Mon Dieu!* Everything is bound to have an explanation,' he says. 'And there's a time for everything. And now the time has come to reveal the truth.'

I don't understand. Have we reached the final scene? He arranges the armchairs of the library suitably. He plans to pace back and forth in front of the fireplace, so he wants the chairs in a semicircle. That way, everyone can see him walking and thinking.

'Are you going to solve our situation?' I ask. I open the curtains a crack.

The detective bows lightly. He takes off his dark overcoat and places it carefully on the back of a chair. Then he adjusts his sleeves and straightens his bow tie. He must feel hot in that outfit. He's even got spats on over his shoes, and it's summer now.

'Dear child. All will be clear once we've got our facts in order,' he assures me. He raises his fat index finger. He looks chubbier in real life than on TV.

'So. Was there frost in the night before the fatality?'

'No way! It was the start of the summer holidays!'

'But there was ice on the ground?'

'Dad said it was glass.'

'But it was ice, *n'est-ce pas*? You felt it with your hand?'

'Yes.'

'*Très intéressant*…An intriguing case!'

The Belgian swivels round and walks in front of the chairs. Then he stops before me and wags his finger.

'You like skiing, don't you?'

'What?'

'You're good at skiing? You were second in a children's skiing race. You used to ski on an icy lake with your mother?'

Sweat gleams on his forehead, but he doesn't stop to wipe it off now, not in the middle of an important scene. I haven't got a clue what he's talking about. It's summer at the moment; wasps are buzzing among the leaves of the creeper and he's just standing there in his spats, gaping.

'Ice fell from the sky! It turned Mum's head into pulp! You know nothing about this!'

'My dear child…'

'Your detective stories don't even have children in them!' I shout. 'They're all grown-ups! You're wrong – you know nothing about this!'

He goes quiet.

'This is a deed committed by an evil man,' he mutters slowly, stroking his moustache. 'We haven't got much time. If my suspicion is correct, we have to get you to a place of safety – and fast. Hastings!' He looks around, but Hastings hasn't yet found his way to the library. 'To the post office! Have the Christmas cards been sent?'

I shake my head.

'You made the cards by hand, *n'est-ce pas*? A snowflake, an elf, an angel, *oui*? I need the addresses – all the addresses! Quite right – you've guessed: the angels! Those cruel messengers. And if it is as I think it is, what I seek is among those addresses!'

The Belgian detective puffs out his chest and pats his sweaty forehead with a handkerchief.

'You've got no idea what this is all about,' I say from behind the curtain.

'Never underestimate –'

'So what's it all about, then?'

He paces back and forth in front of the fireplace again. He wishes he had a bigger audience, you can tell, but we haven't got any guests right now. This is a rubbish final scene. And there's no murder.

'Let's go over the facts: crushed ice on the grass. A skiing race. A mother who disappears. A father who disappears, partially. A child who disappears into a secret room…'

'Even you can't solve this,' I say.

He looks at me for a moment, pinching his moustache.

'There will be a sequel,' he suggests. 'You cannot always cram a mystery into one instalment. The guests don't always fit into one library. Then you need a sequel.'

'No.'

He looks at me. *'Pourquoi pas?'*

'You're useless in this case.'

*'D'accord,'* he says, offended. Then he picks up the coat from the chair, puts it on and again pats his forehead dry with the handkerchief.

'I understand when I am not wanted.' The detective raises his hat a little and walks out.

I hear his footsteps fading in the stairwell.

## 24

And then, one morning, we find Auntie Annu at the kitchen table. She's been sitting there all night, a piece of paper in her hand, glasses on her forehead. Even the kitchen is tired from staying awake all night, what with the burning of lamps and the human breathing. The freezer keeps sighing. It looks as if Auntie's slept part of the night resting on her arm because her cheek's imprinted with the pattern of her jumper.

Dad glances at Auntie but keeps quiet until he's poured out a coffee for himself and some Rice Krispies into a bowl for me. Then he sits down and says, 'Well?'

Auntie Annu glances at Dad, moves the piece of paper she's holding and blinks. When a person is really tired, even her blinking slows down. Then you can really see the blinking happening: the eyes closing and opening again.

Annu passes the piece of paper to Dad and says, 'I won the lottery.'

'That's right.'

'I mean, I won again.'

Auntie scratches her head, finds the glasses on her forehead and pushes them up into her hair.

'2.8 million, cash.'

Dad puts his mug down.

My Rice Krispies crackle in the bowl.

'Why are you still doing the lottery?'

'I've been doing the lottery since I was a student.'

'But you've already won!'

'I can still take part if I want to!' Auntie protests.

'What on earth are you trying to prove?!' Dad shouts, and it's only now I realize this is an argument, though I'm not sure what it's about.

'Exactly! Nothing! You're the one trying to prove some conspiracy theory all the time, staring up at the sky like that, all moody!'

'Be quiet!'

Dad slams down his mug of coffee and stands up with a clatter. He strides to the tired fridge, takes out the fruit juice and sloshes it into a glass, which he slams on the table, shouting all the while.

'It's not going to make it go away, you carrying on doing the lottery and hunting for bargains in shops! Your account is full of money!'

Now Auntie Annu gets up with a clatter, too. She also wants to throw something somewhere, so she grabs the glasses out of her hair and flings them on top of a pile of papers.

'What's that got to do with anything? You're not going to make it go away by lying in bed all summer wearing sunglasses!'

Then Annu and Dad stand in silence for a long time. Annu twists the piece of paper with her fingers.

'Was it the jackpot?' Dad asks in the end.

Auntie Annu nods.

'I didn't know that someone could win twice,' Dad says.

'Well, nor did I, for feck's sake.'

I slurp milk from the bowl and wipe my mouth on my sleeve, but Dad doesn't say anything, even though usually I'm not allowed, because old milk stinks.

'I've got to think about this for a bit,' Auntie Annu says.

Then she and Dad sit down again, looking thoughtful. No one mentions a Jackpot Cake.

'I think I'll go and get some sleep,' Auntie Annu says eventually.

She glances at Dad and a giggle escapes from both of them, which stops as abruptly as it started. Looks like the argument's over.

'Blimey,' Dad says.


And then Auntie climbs up to the room in the tower and falls asleep.

In the afternoon, Dad sends me to ask if Auntie would like to come and have coffee, but Auntie just snores. In the evening, Dad knocks on the door and makes a lot of noise on the steps to the tower, but Auntie doesn't move.

'I wonder if she's got a migraine,' Dad says.

In the morning, Dad goes to shake Auntie, but she just whines, pushes Dad's hand off her shoulder and turns over.

'Are you all right? It's Thursday,' Dad says.

'I'll just sleep for a bit,' Auntie Annu murmurs.

All Dad's attempts to rouse Auntie Annu fail.

Finally, he rings the health centre.

'How am I supposed to bring her there?' Dad snaps into the phone. 'She sleeps in a tower on the second floor. She's heavy!'

Dad's put on hold. He drums his fingers against the kitchen window.

At last the nurse comes back and says a doctor will make a home visit in the afternoon.

'I thought something like this would happen,' Dad mutters to himself.

'Like what?' I ask.

'I don't know,' Dad answers. 'Something serious.'


The doctor listens to Auntie's heart and breathing, pinches her ear and claps his hands, takes a blood sample from Auntie's arm and looks into her eyes with a torch.

Auntie's blood flows along a red pipe into a tube, and I memorize this thought: even when a person's asleep, their blood moves.

'Is it her heart?' Dad asks from the doorway. 'Annu's always eaten quite unhealthily. And we've got a history of heart and circulation problems in our family.'

'Her heart sounds quite normal,' the doctor replies.

'Will you also look into her sugar levels?' Dad continues. 'It just crossed my mind last night it could be sugar.'

'Did anything particular happen before she fell asleep?'

'A lottery win,' Dad answers.

The doctor raises his eyebrows. He doesn't say anything at first.

'For the second time,' I say from behind Dad.

'That's right,' Dad mutters.

'I see,' the doctor answers.

'She didn't fall asleep when she won the first time,' I explain. 'We all had cake then.'

'That's right,' Dad says.

'In that case, it's probably a reaction induced by a shock,' the doctor said. 'The mind needs a rest and battens down the hatches, as it were. Let her sleep. She'll wake up when she's ready. Put a glass of fruit juice and some easy-to-digest food on the bedside table once a day.'

Then the doctor leaves.


And so Auntie Annu sleeps on. We bring her juice, rusks and jelly. Auntie eats and drinks in her sleep. Sometimes she even opens her eyes a little, but they're drowsy and vacant. Auntie bites a rusk, turns over and sinks into sleep, crumbs on her lips.

## 25

So I'm all alone now. Auntie sleeps, Dad fixes the barn ceiling, Mum's dead and the summer holidays aren't over yet.

Dad cooks bad food, like sausages still frozen on the inside. He can't make pancakes, either. He gets a recipe off the internet, but the result is still a pulpy mess. We eat greasy, sugar-coated pancake-pulp.

Dad huffs, annoyed. 'Must have been a bad recipe. I did everything just like it said. And these pans of Annu's! Why doesn't she buy new pots and pans, what with all that money she's got? But then, there've been none on special offer anywhere. Still, they taste kind of…Don't you think they taste like pancakes, Saara?'

'I suppose.'

Dad takes to banging his feet against the bars of the bed again, and the doctor grants him more sick leave. Dad forgets to enrol me for swimming lessons; I was supposed to learn front crawl this summer. By way of consolation, he buys me a bagful of autumn clothes.

I stand in front of the mirror in a new turquoise shirt. My wrists poke out of the sleeves. The legs of the jeans are long enough, but I can't do the button up.

'They're quite nice, aren't they?' Dad says, looking at my mirror image.

I turn to face him, then tear off the clothes. The shirt collar is so tight I can barely get my head out. Hasn't he bothered to look at me all summer?

'Stupid! You can't do anything right!' I shout, marching out of the room.

I'm so annoyed I don't talk to Dad all evening. Even though he's made macaroni bake for tea. The macaroni is hard and white. It stands on the plate, a cube cut out with a knife.

# 26

Auntie's sheep are in the pasture. They smell of Auntie Annu, and that gives me a cosy feeling. I sink my hands into Bruno's brown, or black, wool and stroke his head. He twitches his ears, one straight, the other one wonky, to shoo away flies. Bruno has become an ordinary sheep, and he can't comfort me. He still follows me, but he's stopped skipping and being a sweet, funny lamb. Now he's boring, and looks as stupid as the other sheep in the enclosure. He chews grass and dashes around.

Auntie once said that she can't eat mutton. According to Auntie, sheep is the only animal whose butchered meat smells the same as the living animal. A pork chop doesn't smell of pig, minced beef doesn't smell of cow, but a rack of lamb smells of sheep. And that's why Auntie Annu won't touch lamb casserole.

I don't know if the sheep have noticed Auntie Annu's absence. They have stupid eyes, their mouths chew stupidly away, they're startled by the smallest thing and they fire out droppings without even noticing it. One day, a white sheep got caught in the barbed-wire fence. There it stood, having been there all night, for all I knew, looking as if it had decided to lose all hope and die.

When I got there, the sheep took fright and gave a small, startled skip. And that little skip was enough to free the wool from the barbed wire and so the sheep ran back to the others as if nothing had happened. I looked at it and thought: you could have made a bit of an effort, if that was all it took. But sheep don't really do effort.

I scratch Bruno's neck. I've heard that there's a spot on every sheep's neck that is so itchy that the animal just has to lift its head higher and higher if you scratch it there. And when a sheep looks up long enough, blood stops flowing to its brain and it passes out.

I see if I can make Bruno pass out. I scratch his neck, looking for the itchy spot. After a couple of attempts, I do manage to make his head rise. Bruno's eyes stare up at the sky, but then he suddenly turns and slips through my fingers. He skips round once and comes back for more scratching.

I try again. The scratching has to be carried out with just the right amount of force. If it's too light, the head doesn't go up; if it's too heavy, Bruno will run off. I scratch; Bruno raises his head.

The fourth attempt is going well. Bruno's brown head stretches up higher and higher; I scratch and scratch. And at last, unexpectedly, Bruno slumps to my feet, unconscious.

I stare at the passed-out sheep. His eyes are open, and you can see his teeth in his mouth, which gapes a little. A moment goes by, then Bruno comes to. He stands up, skips sideways, runs to a stone and back, then returns to me.

Don't you understand anything, thicko? I ask in my head, stroking Bruno behind his wonky ear. But he doesn't understand. He doesn't understand, and he can't offer comfort. He has a hard, bony skull, and nothing hurts him. I've heard that you can hit a sheep on the head with your fist, and all that happens is your knuckles get bruised.

Auntie Annu doesn't wake up. She's been asleep for two weeks now and has stopped eating the snacks we've been leaving her. She still drinks a little water. She seems to have sunk into a deeper sleep than last week. Her breathing is slow and even, and she doesn't change positions as often as she did in the beginning. The doctor visits again, but he can't wake Auntie up, either. He thinks she can sleep if she feels like sleeping. But in a week's time, she'll be taken into hospital for drip-feeding if she's still not eating.

I'm a bit worried about Auntie Annu's teeth. She hasn't brushed them for days, and she's eaten biscuits and jelly. If Dad remembered to buy xylitol pastilles, I could leave them out for Auntie, but he doesn't remember anything.

I sit on the floor of the secret room. Usually, I sit here and think about the pieces of Mum, but this time, I pretend I'm walled in. This room isn't surrounded by any line; this room is as free as a line between things. Here you can imagine you're a white sheep stuck to a fence, preparing for a slow death.

'Saara? Food's ready.' It's Dad's voice in the passage.

But the walled-in girl and the sheep stuck to the fence are so weak by now that they haven't got the strength to answer.

'Saara!' Dad's voice rises then grows more distant as he walks back to the stairwell. 'Where are you?'

The girl is inside a wall. The sheep hangs from barbed wire. Auntie sleeps, unconscious, in the tower. Bruno lies in the grass, passed out.

The girl has been shouting for a while, but now her strength has gone and all she can do is lie and listen to the bleating of the sheep. All evening she also hears the calls of her idiot Dad but she doesn't feel like wasting her last bit of energy on answering him. There she lies, her wool tangled in barbs, and waits.

*Once upon a time, there was a prince whom a witch changed into a frog. The prince's disappearance was mourned by his servant Bruno. Bruno mourned so hard that, eventually, three iron hoops were needed to compress his heart and prevent it from breaking.*

*One day, the prince changed back into a human being and found himself a princess. The pair jumped into a carriage driven by Bruno and travelled towards the prince's castle. Three times during the journey, a loud metallic bang rang out. The prince and princess thought the carriage was falling apart, but Bruno told them that the sound was only his heart being freed from the hoops of grief.*

*And that's the end of that.*

# THE FIVE LIGHTNING
# STRIKES OF HAMISH MACKAY

Hamish MacKay was born fifty-eight years ago in the village of Crossbost on the island of Lewis in the Outer Hebrides. He owns a fishing boat and catches lobsters and crabs for a living.

Hamish MacKay has only left his village four times: once with the school as a sixth-former, to go to Glasgow; once to attend his sister's wedding; once to buy a van. And when his wife Mary had her fiftieth, Hamish MacKay and Mary sent off for passports and flew to Thailand for a fortnight.

Thailand was hot. Breakfast involved the same sort of food as lunch and dinner did, and bread was nowhere to be had. For souvenirs, Hamish bought a T-shirt adorned with a map of Thailand, a tortoise shell and decorative dolls dressed in glittering clothes. Then he and Mary came back home.


Our story begins on a Sunday evening in 1988. The wind changed direction, to the north-east, thunder rumbled above the sea, and rain clouds gathered on the horizon.

Hamish MacKay decided a couple more ropes were needed on the boat. He walked to the sea, noticing that the landscape had turned yellow. The wind filled his ears. Suddenly, all colour vanished and the sea sank into darkness, though it was only six o'clock.

The first lightning struck and lit up the open sea. In the light, Hamish saw small, sharp, hissing ripples on the surface of the water, as in a film shown at high speed. The wind rose so fast that not even the waves could keep up. Darkness returned, and Hamish ran to the boat, which was tossing restlessly between the buoy and the shore, a green bucket clattering along its deck. Hamish jumped on to the deck, attached the extra ropes, shut the trapdoor securely and put the bucket inside.

It began raining. The water poured over him like a waterfall and made the ground steam. It had been a hot week.

As Hamish MacKay was starting back, lightning struck. Like a bright, fiery nail, it pinned him down. The whole landscape exploded.

Darkness returned, and Hamish was lying there, limbs trembling uncontrollably, momentarily incapable of any action. His hair had been burnt, and his boots had flown off his feet. His muscles were struck by cramp and his pulse throbbed in his throat. Nevertheless, he remained conscious. The boots turned up later among the stones on the shore.

Without hair, eyelashes or shoes, Hamish staggered home and asked Mary to give him a glass of milk. Mary stared at her husband, who smelled of electricity and burnt hair, and rushed out to start the car.

Mary drove Hamish to the hospital in Stornoway. They examined the man's heart, memory and soles. No serious injuries were found, and Hamish MacKay went back the following morning to clean his bait fish.

During the August storms of 1992, lightning struck for the second time. Hamish MacKay and his fishing companion Timothy McCallum managed to shelter from the storm close to a nearby island, but lightning struck the boat's aerial. Electrical discharge ran down the sides of the boat and spread along the metal railings over the whole vessel. Hamish burnt his hand on the aft rail. But Tim flew into the sea, propelled by the lightning, and drowned. His body was only found two days later, having drifted into the next bay along.

The boat's interior was totally destroyed by fire. Fittings flew off the walls, windows exploded, gauges and other electrical equipment splintered apart. Plastics melted, wood burnt. Black, dirty water lapped at the floor, and the air was acrid with the smell of burning. A jagged line, branded by lightning, ran across the whole of the wood-panelled wall. The bucket taken in by Hamish had melted to form a green blob on the cabin floor.

After Tim McCallum's funeral, rumours began circulating in the village. Someone said Hamish MacKay must have done some wrong and been punished. Others felt he thought too highly of himself – he'd started learning French – while others still brought up that old quarrel between Hamish and his old man. People also saw fit to speculate as to why he and his blone had no wee ones, and why Hamish's hair had turned white after the first strike.

Mary and Hamish carried on with their lives as best they could. Hamish bought a new, smaller trawler and named it *Silver Darling*. His white hair and eyebrows grew back.

None of the village men dared go out to sea with Hamish any more. He and Mary had to manage by themselves.

The third time lightning struck Hamish MacKay was in 1995 when he was mending the garden shed behind the cottage. This time the bang was so loud that Mary rushed out to the back, hearing it. She saw the neighbour's horse first. It was running in fright, pulling a cart behind it. One of the wheels sank into a ditch and made the cart tilt. The cart got stuck and the horse reared and was propelled on to its side by the impact of this abrupt stop. From the garden, Mary could see the whites of the animal's eyes, glinting in the dusk. The neighbour was somewhere in the background, running and calling for his horse, but that Mary didn't see.

Hamish MacKay was standing at the edge of the garden. The same smell of burning wafted around him. His hair was scorched again. It had burnt part of his scalp. His eyebrows and eyelashes had disappeared, too. The nails had come off his fingers.

Mary tried to talk to her husband, but he didn't reply. He just stood there on the spot, swaying, his gaze wandering round the garden. He didn't seem to recognize his wife. Then he staggered to the water butt and dunked his head in its contents. Immediately afterwards, he passed out.

In the hospital bed, Hamish stared at his wife with vacant, lashless eyes. He wouldn't let anyone touch him: if someone tried, he would scream instantly. The lightest touch seemed to hurt, as if a layer of skin had been burnt clean off. Mary suspected briefly that Hamish had lost his reason, but examinations revealed that her husband had in fact lost his hearing.

This time, Hamish MacKay was a changed man. The joy drained out of him; with deafness came gloom. Hamish MacKay sank into silence.

The villagers grew afraid of both Hamish and his wife. People shunned them in stormy weather. The gossip had stopped, and so had theories about Hamish's sins. People just shook their heads and fell silent.

But life went on. The blone cleaned the cod and the mackerel. The cove chopped up the waste and put it in the lobster traps. They laid the traps together in the sea and took them out two days later. They sold the lobsters and crabs to a supplier in Stornoway.

Lightning struck for the fourth time in 2007 as Hamish MacKay was returning home from his ma's funeral. His Sunday suit caught fire and a burn the shape of tree roots marked his back. It zigzagged from his right shoulder to his left hip. This time, the nerves in his left leg were also damaged. Hamish developed a limp. His hair and nails grew back. His posture collapsed.

By 2012, Hamish MacKay had been struck by lightning more times than any other European. In global terms, he was number four for all time. He got a mention in *Guinness World Records*.

Hamish MacKay featured in an episode of a documentary series made by the BBC. The programme analysed the frequency of thunderstorms in the Outer Hebrides and compared Hamish to other fishermen working in the area. The case of Hamish MacKay remained a mystery to the programme makers.

Dear Mr MacKay,

I watched the documentary about you on television, and your story touched me greatly. I wanted to write to you because fate has also toyed with me. It is true my case is very different from yours, and involves no thunder. I have won the lottery twice, you see. (And you are the only person outside my family whom I have told.) Maybe after four lightning strikes you think two wins is not a big deal, but in any case, I have been thrown off course quite badly.

I hope you do not mind if I tell my story. Three years ago, I won the lottery. What a coincidence – my exact numbers in those plastic tubes! Incredible! But on the other hand, somebody's numbers always drop into the tubes, and this time they just happened to be mine.

I settled my debts and arranged my life exactly as I wanted.
I did some travelling. I bought an old house. I had the perfect
workshop built. I was happy! Everything had been sorted
out! Do you understand, Mr MacKay? I had been short of
money all my life, and now all those worries were gone.
What a sense of freedom, and what a relief!

But then I had another win. Again my numbers dropped
into the tubes – different numbers from the first time. I did
not know that was even possible, but there they were. And
suddenly chance did not seem a good enough explanation.
I was not happy and I did not rejoice. I did not feel anything
at all. In some strange way, this second win took away the
pleasure that the first one had granted.

I was struck by a strange sense of guilt. As if I had been
caught playing with something without permission. But I had
not done anything wrong! I have always bought a lottery ticket;
I did not want to stop. I like the excitement of the draw. I like
the way the balls drop down. Very little else in life is so regular.

I thought: life goes on. I live, I do my felting, I buy my
lottery ticket, I get things when they are on special offer in
the supermarket.

But I feel now that this must be about something else.
But what, exactly?

Am I the butt of some kind of joke?

What will happen next?

Then I happened to see the documentary about you on
television, and I thought, that man will surely understand

my situation. That man had a brush with fate, just like me. Perhaps he can give me an answer.

The BBC was not willing to give me your address but a kind production secretary has promised to forward this letter. I will put my contact details below.

Best wishes,
Annu Heiskanen

●●●●●●●

Dear Mrs Heiskanen,

I'm a fisherman by trade. I catch lobsters and crabs, and I live in a wee cottage with my wife. In our garden we grow runner beans, potatoes, three kinds of cabbage and pumpkins.

You ask for an explanation but you'll have to find one yourself, I'm afraid, because in my experience, what others say won't help.

Regards,
Hamish MacKay
PS my address is below.

Dear Mr MacKay,

Forgive me for writing again. I do understand that I have to solve this myself. But you seemed so calm in the documentary, and I was left wondering: are you not afraid, or annoyed? I am furious, myself! Or I would be, if I knew where to direct my fury.

It is not very often a person can draw a line on a calendar to demonstrate the exact point at which her life changed. But you and I, Mr MacKay, we can. One could argue that I have been trapped by good fortune, and you by misfortune, but it is not that simple. Listen, the rug can be pulled out from under your feet with no suffering involved. That is why I wrote to you and why I write again. Forgive me. I am just so alone with this.

Regards,
Annu Heiskanen

●●●●●●●

Dear Mrs Heiskanen,

Believe me, I've also asked: is this a joke? What does it mean? But those questions don't get me anywhere, and that's why I've stopped asking.

My wife Mary planted the runner-bean seedlings in the vegetable patch. A bean rises out of the soil all feisty and green and bursting with confidence. For a moment it sways by itself like a bairn learning to walk, but as soon as it touches something, it wraps itself round it with its hairy stalk, looking for support. It has such blind faith in strangers.

And do you know, Mrs Heiskanen, we're not completely on our own? I read in the *Reader's Digest* that a forester living in the United States was struck by lightning seven times. After the seventh time he shot himself in the head with a shotgun. And I for one can't judge him for it.

Kind regards,
Hamish MacKay

● ● ● ● ● ● ●

Dear Mr MacKay,

I nearly came to grief, though I did not grab a shotgun. I fell asleep. After the second lottery win, I slept for three and a half weeks, nearly forgetting to wake up.

While asleep, I did not dream. I remember sinking into sleep; I fell into something deep and dark, and three and a half weeks later I surfaced again. My brother and his daughter claim that I ate and blinked, and in the first few days I even spoke a sentence or two – I have no memory of this myself.

When I woke up, I felt heavy, rather like after a rainy night. I do not know about you, Mr MacKay, but my sleep is always very deep on rainy nights. Someone was reading aloud: horse-racing results. At first I did not understand where the voice was coming from, but then I saw that a radio had been brought into the room. My brother had decided to play the news, weather forecasts and lottery results for me every day. Maybe to make fun of me, I am not sure.

I stood up and promptly fell against a chair. My head was spinning and my stomach was turning. I tottered down the stairs, barely able to support myself on the banister. My brother and his daughter heard my clattering, luckily, and came to meet me. Together they managed to lead me downstairs.

I sat at the table and tried to work out what my brother and the girl were saying. I riffled through the mail and newspapers piled on the table and it was only then that I realized I really had slept non-stop for twenty-five days and nights.

I had not washed for almost a month and the girl wrinkled her nose. But I was too weak to stand up in the shower, so my brother ordered me to sit on a plastic stool and the girl to be on standby at the door.

After the shower, I began to eat. It seemed I would never cease. During the first twenty-four hours, I ate everything. The girl giggled when my stomach rumbled and purred like a herd of cats.

That was five months ago.

What was it that woke me up? Was it a thought, was it hunger or did I simply realize that I did not want to die, after all?

Mr MacKay, have you been able to explain to yourself what has kept you alive?

Regards,
Annu Heiskanen

•••••••••

Dear Mrs Heiskanen,

Your letters have not gone unnoticed. Today the postman joked I was a famous TV star, what with getting fan mail now: from abroad, even. It's given them something to talk about in the post office.

I don't get out much these days. The third lightning strike destroyed my hearing. I can't say I've missed listening to people talk that much. I speak to Mary as I always have done, and I can lip-read, though that's not easy in the boat. I've got to keep my eyes on the trap and my wife's lips at the same time. Signing doesn't always work, either, not with your fingers caught up in the string of a trap. But we understand a lot without the need for words.

Sometimes I wish I could still hear the wind. I hadn't realized how much I could tell about the weather with my hearing. Now I have to open the door and feel the direction of the wind on my face. In the boat, the blone complains when the engine gets too noisy. I must admit that when I'm at sea, I don't miss my hearing. I never liked coves who talk while fishing. Never mind sing. And the waves, those you just feel. I just hope I don't lose my sight.

You wrote of a sleep so deep it had no dreams. For me, too, when the lightning strikes, there is an emptiness. For a moment I remember nothing; everything gets wiped away. Then, when the charge is gone, I remember again and the pain comes. But the emptiness, that's dizzying.

I don't know why I haven't died. The people here say it's in punishment, but they don't say that aloud, not any more. Not since Mary gave them a piece of her mind.

Hamish MacK

• • • • • • •

Hello Mr MacKay,

I still haven't claimed my second lottery win. I'm afraid if this gets out, someone will have the bright idea of contacting the papers and I'll become a celebrity freak. I'm afraid the girl will tell people at school, or somebody will guess down at the shop, anything.

I don't dare do the lottery any more.

You've just carried on as you always have, isn't that right? Aren't you scared?

I'm totally listless, somehow; I just sit and mull things over. I feel there's something I simply don't understand.

My whole life is split in two. Part of me functions as before: wakes up, walks, eats. But in the shop I just stand there. The person next to me in the aisle probably won't have any idea that the woman beside them has lost the plot. But as I stand there thinking, it feels as if the goods are falling off the shelves on top of me, or the floor is disappearing. Then I pay, gather my shopping into my bag and drive home like any ordinary person.

My brother is having a hard time of it; I can't talk to him. Yesterday, I tried to look up the contact details of the national lottery on the internet, but I ended up staring foolishly at the browser. I wrote: *what help lotto*. Then I had a sudden thought, which woke me up: I wish I were a sheep! I said to myself, 'baa', and it felt good, in a jolly sort of way. I typed *baa* into the browser. I felt like running outside to join the flock in the front garden.

Annu

•••••••

Dear Mrs Heiskanen,

A terrible storm has been raging for three days now: I've not been able to go out to sea. Three slates came off the roof and a piece of the guttering as well.

The *Silver Darling* is a wee thing, and I don't want to go out if the gale force is more than 15 m/s. When the wind tosses them around, the traps get covered in sludge.

I went out on the bicycle yesterday, and the wind was so strong that I had to pedal even going downhill. Not enough that uphill was hard going! It's always dreich here, and windy. There are no trees, nor anything else. Just rock. Rock in the sea, rock on land. But to have to pedal downhill!

I went to the post office. There was a queue because people were waiting for a delivery from the bakery. As soon as I walked in, everyone stopped talking, as usual. They looked at me for a split second and then out the window at the clouds in the sky.

A lot of people think I'm cursed. Or that God is testing me, like Job in the Old Testament. According to rumour, I ran home from the shore after the third lightning strike because a thundercloud was following me and I wanted to keep my new boat from being wrecked. They say I kept swerving, trying to trick the cloud, but it just kept on coming after me. Then, when it finally struck, the neighbour's horse bolted, got injured and had to be shot.

That isn't true, of course. I didn't think then (and I don't think now) that clouds, the sky or God were chasing me or anybody else.

I stopped going to church after the third time. I wasn't that much of a churchgoer before then, but if lightning strikes me three times and leaves the kirk standing on top of the cliff, I've lost interest in anything the minister might have to say about it.

For some, it's easier to think that God is punishing a sinner. Och, well. Others believe in miracles. I'm not quite sure what's meant by talk about miracles. People seem to think that if some mysterious event is a miracle, then there's an explanation for it. That the event itself may be impossible to fathom but the fact that it happened means some kind of message is behind it.

Perhaps the world needs shaking up from time to time, Mrs Heiskanen. I've certainly shaken up this village. When I go into the shop, one look at me reminds all the customers that at any moment, the sky can fall on top of us.

Your friend Hamish MacKay

● ● ● ● ● ● ●●

Hello,

Spring is round the corner where we are. The evenings are getting lighter, the snow is melting, and the sheep gambol wildly outside the house.

You stated in your second letter that we are not alone, and you told me about the American forester. But you know what, Mr MacKay, there are others, too!

Sometimes the sky falls; sometimes the earth sinks. Sometimes you are struck by such an incredible piece of luck that it is hard to carry on.

Sometimes something happens – just that once – but for the rest of your life you have to wonder why. Sometimes nothing happens, and for the rest of your life you wonder why it didn't.

But now, stories. My brother told me about a shipwreck. He has been very interested in calculating probability lately, and that is how he came across this story. I wrote it down for you.

A MOTHER'S LUCK

In September 1940, the steamer SS *Duchess of Kent* left Liverpool for Canada. It was carrying 139 children. The English were afraid of a German landing, and many families sent their children abroad, to safety, including across the ocean to the United States and Canada. On 26 September, a German U-boat sank the *Duchess of Kent* with two torpedoes. When the cargo ship HMS *Albert* arrived at the scene, eight hours later, it found two surviving boys on a raft, and, a little later, a girl drifting on her own in a lifeboat.

The children were taken back to England, where the whole country mourned the fate of the dead children. As a result of the disaster, the transport of children overseas was abandoned.

But one mother was lucky. Because, of the three children who survived out of the 139 passengers on the ship, two were hers. Her son and daughter had both made it to their own life raft, unaware of the other's fate. Seventy-six families sent their children to safety, and this mother was the only one who didn't lose either of her children (the two sisters of the other surviving boy drowned).

The family withdrew into isolation. After the war, they emigrated to the United States, and the mother never consented to talk to the media about what had happened.

Mr MacKay, I am sure you can understand why the fate of this mother touches me. What a mightily disproportionate piece of luck! How could the mother explain to herself why it was that *her* children had made it? Well, perhaps she couldn't, seeing that she moved to another continent. Did her children possess a special tenacity, a will to live? Or perhaps they were merely more ruthless than the others. Did the mother have to ask herself that question? *Did my children make it because they pushed others out of the way?*

Unfortunately, the woman in question is dead now. But I wanted to share her story with you.

I hope there are enough lobsters in the sea and the winds remain calm. I shall look for more stories and write to you again!

Very best wishes
Annu

●●●●●●●

Hello Mrs Heiskanen,

You asked me if I'm ever afraid. I've thought it over: a tricky one, that.

My first thought was: if I let fear take over, what would I be left with? No work, no freedom, nothing. I've got to live as I always have done.

But of course I'm afraid. Not so much for me as for Mary. Not that I can say that to her.

When there's thunder in the air, I leave home. I make up something I've got to do: on the shore, around the shed or somewhere else I can be alone. After Tim's death, I don't want to have another accident on my conscience.

It's not something I do knowingly. Last time there was a storm, I was tidying a pile of driftwood in the woodshed when suddenly, there was Mary, standing in front of me, shouting. She'd probably been shouting at me for a while, but, of course, I can't hear. She tried to drag me indoors, and I fought her off. It became quite a scrap.

That time neither of us came to any harm. We sat in the woodshed all evening, just cuddling.

Hamish M.

●●●●●●●

Dearest Mr MacKay,

I watched a short film on the computer. It was made in 1978, in Puerto Rico, and shows Karl Wallenda, the famous tight-rope walker, falling and dying during a live television pro-gramme. The whole sequence lasts a mere twenty seconds but there is something so fascinating about it that I have watched it over and over again.

Karl Wallenda belonged to a well-known circus family. These days, his great-grandson walks between skyscrapers and crosses the Niagara Falls. But in 1978, Karl Wallenda walked at an altitude of thirty-seven metres with the aim of getting from one ten-storey building to another. Then, all of a sudden, he was caught by a gust of wind and the cable began to swing. The film shows him trying to crouch down, grabbing hold of the cable with one hand. But his foot failed to hook on to the cable, missing it, and Karl Wallenda fell. So mundanely, so fumblingly, like any of us. And before the bystanders had time to take it in properly, Karl Wallenda had hit the street.

There are people who defy danger for so long that I suppose you start believing in their immortality. Some who are so skilled that they must have magic powers or a supernatural ability. And children always have a guardian angel accompanying them. But in the end, all it takes is a single gust of wind, one stupid slip, and a person just dies.

Annu

• • • • • • •

Dearest Mrs Heiskanen,

As a lad I went fishing with my uncle. My cousin Graham was younger than me and couldn't manage all the things that needed doing – I was stronger and better with my hands. Once, we were at sea and the waves were coming thick and fast. We were heading out to the open sea, Uncle trying to press on, looking for a course that meant the waves wouldn't hit the boat full on. But it was rocking wildly.

I heard Uncle shouting he was going to turn around. He managed to bear off slightly when, out of nowhere, a wave washed right over the deck. My cousin Graham vanished; I saw it happening. Just one movement, just one moment. Graham didn't utter a single sound. The sea rolled round twice, and it was all over. Graham had disappeared.

We combed the surroundings for a long time. A couple of other boats came to help us. We were tossed by the waves and the wind pushed us towards the shore, but there was no sign of Graham. I don't know if you've ever tried to look at the sea when it's rough; it's impossible to see into all its pleats and folds.

That's when I understood, for the first time, how beyond our ken the sea is. It has no memory or conscience. Lightning bolts are somewhat like that as well. They are not pursuing me. They don't remember where they've struck previously – they're not interested, either.

Your friend Hamish MacKay

My dear friend Mr MacKay,

I hope you are well. I have spent the past few weeks doing up the house. I started restoring the downstairs rooms to their original state. I hired a master carpenter for the job.

We have discovered twelve layers of wallpaper on some of the walls and five layers of backing paper on the ceiling. I bought a chandelier for the drawing room at auction. The original drawing-room chandelier was itself sold at auction at some point, as was the bulk of the furniture. It was quite a project to transport a chandelier over a metre in length here in a van, never mind clean it one crystal at a time... Well, now it glitters there.

Apart from the building work, everyday life continues to be a struggle. If I am honest, I only started the whole restoration business in order to achieve something. But now the workmen are doing everything, and I am only called to the scene when there is a problem or when a decision needs to be made. A couple of times I went to ask if an extra pair of hands was needed or if I could do something, but they don't want me.

When I go to the workshop, I just stare at the wool and stand there. I forget to go shopping, the car will not start because I forgot to have it MOT'd. Before the summer holidays began, I once forgot to pick the girl up from school. I only woke up when someone from the after-school club rang to say there was a girl there from class 3C and was someone going to collect her?

I am fifty-four as of yesterday. I stood outside watching the fireworks bought by my brother and I couldn't find it in myself to be happy. What will happen next year? The girl was hopping about, all enthusiastic about the fireworks, but I would have liked to go and hide indoors.

I found another couple of new stories and decided to write to you straight away. The first is a sports item(!), the other happens at sea again.

THE PERFECT JUMP

When Bob Beamon took part in the men's long jump at the 1968 summer Olympics, his personal best was 8.33 metres and so he was one of the front runners in the competition.

The first two rounds failed to yield a result because Beamon overstepped both times. On his third attempt, he performed well and got into the final.

In the final, Beamon executed a jump that reached the other end of the sandy area. It even overshot the field covered by the optical measuring device, so the distance had to be calculated manually.

It turned out to be 8.9 metres.

This improved the long jump world record by over half a metre; previous increases since 1901 had averaged 6 centimetres.

When the announcer read out the length of the jump, Beamon himself did not understand it because he was used to imperial measurements. When a teammate translated the result for him, Beamon fell to his knees, face buried in his hands, because he was suffering a momentary cataplectic fit.

Shortly after the jump, it began pouring down at the stadium, making the job of the other finalists more difficult. The East German who got silver jumped 8.19 metres.

And this is the bit you will like, Mr MacKay: one sports reporter called Beamon a man who had seen lightning. Never had he jumped more than 8.33 metres before his Olympic achievement and never would he jump more than 8.22 metres after those games. Just that once he succeeded in producing the perfect jump.

Bob Beamon's world record remained in place for twenty-three years and is still the world's second-best result today.


A SEA RESCUE


In 2014, a fibreglass boat drifted to an atoll in the Pacific Ocean. The boat was all scratched up and covered with mussels and other marine creatures. The following items were discovered inside: a waterfowl chick, still alive; a dead turtle; turtle shells; remnants of fish – and a thin, bearded, long-haired man clad only in a pair of threadbare underpants.

The man was led ashore. He appeared to know only Spanish and when, having drunk a couple of glasses of water, he began to talk, he kept repeating to himself, 'I feel bad, very bad, I am very far away...'

He was extremely thin and confused.

The occupants of the atoll included a Norwegian marine scientist and some local inhabitants. At first, there was no one there who spoke Spanish. The man was taken to the mayor. He introduced himself as José Ivan and said he had set out from Mexico sixteen months earlier. But Mexico was 13,000 kilometres away.

José Ivan drew the mayor a picture. It showed a boat, with two men inside it. Then he drew an arrow to demonstrate that one of the men had fallen from the boat into the water. He drew turtles, birds and fish. He drew his own hands. He drew rain and turtle blood. He drew a light falling from the sky and a horse running alongside water. He drew children dancing in water with turtle shells. He drew till the point of the pencil snapped.

The researchers doubted José Ivan's story. It transpired that José Ivan was a made-up name (the man appeared to have been living in Mexico illegally). It also seemed impossible for him to have drifted 13,000 kilometres in his small boat.

I found a photo of José Ivan on the internet. It had been taken two weeks after his landing. The man's hair is short again and his beard has been shaved off. His skin is blotchy and seems to have peeled off in places. The expression in his eyes is joyless. And, Mr MacKay, guess what José Ivan says, according to the caption? 'I just want to be left in peace.'

Wishing you a good winter.
Annu

• • • • • • •

Dear Mrs Heiskanen,

I laughed a lot, reading José Ivan's story. The man drifts at sea for almost a year and a half, on his own, mostly, not knowing if he'll ever make it ashore alive, and when he's finally rescued, he says, 'I just want to be left in peace'!

As for everyday life, only you can do it. You and I, we know it's all make-believe. But it's still not worth giving up on altogether. That's what I think. Every day I go to my boat, though I know it's not really important. Then again, what else have I got? If I weren't fishing, what else would there be?

Best wishes,
Hamish M.

My friend Mr MacKay,

Thank you for your latest letter; it was a great help to me. The very next morning I went to my workshop, tidied up and set to work. I started simply: pot holders! They are nicely rectangular, clear in every way. (Find one enclosed within.) A rectangle is a pleasant shape, isn't it? Anything you can contain within four corners is clear. A little like the frame of a painting. In fact, all the things I make – carpets, wall hangings, pictures, pot holders – are rectangular. Now that I think of it, the rectangle is my favourite shape of all time.

My niece plays at murder mysteries. She appears to be obsessed with the business of bodies. Lately she has been asking me to draw a line round her. She lies down on the floor, sprawls there as if she has just been stabbed in the back and demands I draw round her with chalk. It is really important to her that the line is unbroken and reflects her actual size. Then she stands up, examines the figure, walks to the other end of the room and dies again. Our library upstairs is currently littered with bodies.

Annu

PS the story I am sending this time is from a newspaper. You might think it is not relevant but I could not get it out of my mind. Not so much what happened, but why.

A WRESTLING MATCH

Jürgen fell out with his school friends. The boys started wrestling, and Jürgen lost. He was annoyed but went with his friends to a bar. Then he decided to leave, and ran home. He grabbed his father's guns and returned to the town centre on his scooter.

Jürgen climbed on to a shop roof and sat down. He listened to some music on his phone, and when the track ended, he looked at the street below through the sight of a small-bore rifle. 'After watching for a while, I began shooting,' Jürgen explained to the judge.

Jürgen fired twenty shots with the small-bore rifle but when no one seemed to take any notice, he swapped it for a hunting rifle. He only stopped when he saw two men fall to the ground.

'Then I ran off. I suddenly got the feeling I wanted to go to sleep,' Jürgen says. He slept in the woods for a while and then walked home. When he saw the police in front of his house, he went to sit down by the side of the road. That's where the police found him.

In court, Jürgen was asked why he began shooting.

'Well, 'cause I lost the wrestling match,' he answered. 'That's all I can say.'

My friend Hamish MacKay,

Greetings from Kyoto; I decided to go on a little trip.

The building works seemed to be getting on fine without me, and I was beginning to get fed up with the pot holders. My brother, who was ill all summer, is feeling a bit better now and is back at work. My niece goes to school by bus now, on her own, so I thought it safe to go away for a while.

The card shows a park I visited yesterday. The tea I had to drink there was over a hundred years old. Can you imagine!

I hope you are well. Perhaps you have written during my absence and a letter awaits me at home.

Regards from your friend Annu

• • • • • • •

Dear Mr MacKay,

These are the boats they use to fish with in Okinawa! I ate lobster yesterday, and when I saw this card on a stand, I decided to send it to you. I wonder if your letter has got lost in the post; my brother said on the phone that no letter has arrived.

Warm wishes,
Annu

My dear friend,

The first snow has fallen in Finland. It is equally magical every time. Now everything is clean and white, the evenings don't feel dark and all the unfinished jobs in the garden have been mercifully covered by snow. We shall have to see how long the snow will stay. They have forecast milder weather for next week, which here in the south means a return to slush and darkness. I never got round to tidying the edges of the sand path before the end of autumn, damn it. It takes several days to straighten them with a spade. But what can you do? A lawnmower is no good for that job.

In *The New York Times* they gave out on the aeroplane I found the story of Tom Sanders. I was going to send you the whole cutting but I may have accidentally made a compost bag out of it. I record the story here as I remember it.

THE EARTH SWALLOWED UP A SLEEPING MAN

28.2.2013, Florida (if I remember rightly). Tom Sanders went to bed at night, as usual. His wife was working the night shift and the children were asleep in their rooms, upstairs from their parents'. At 2.14 a.m., the ground under Tom Sanders's house unexpectedly gave way. A ten-metre chasm opened up, drawing in the bedroom floor, along with the room's sleeping occupant, Tom Sanders.

The children ran downstairs and saw that half of the bottom floor of the house was missing. The neighbours alerted the authorities, who managed to rescue the children from the stairs. The search for Tom Sanders, who had been swallowed up by the ground, began immediately. The family hoped he was caught in a kind of air pocket.

Twenty-four hours later, the search had to be discontinued because the whole house was in danger of collapsing. The man was never found. The depth of the subsidence was estimated at around ten metres but could not be assessed with any certainty.

So if the sky and the sea are not reliable, then neither, always, is the ground! Lumps of ice fall, lightning strikes, waves surge, and sometimes the ground quite simply tears itself open.

I hope you are well and looking after yourself.

Regards,
Annu Heiskanen

●●●●●●●

My friend Mr MacKay,

I wish you a merry Christmas. I trust you have not changed address?

I forgot to tell you in my previous letter about a woman who was sitting next to me on the plane, a retiree. Mrs Judith said that sometimes, what's most miraculous is when nothing happens. She told me about how, in 1999, she was almost the victim of a bomb attack.

She was standing at a supermarket checkout when there was a bang by the shop entrance. The security guard standing in the doorway was hit by a cluster of nails and lost both of his eyes. Many others were injured, too. But Mrs Judith was bagging her shopping, ten seconds away from the door.

I said it was lucky that nothing happened to her.

So everyone said, she replied. Nothing happened. That's true. But for years she kept asking herself:

Why was I in that particular place?

Why wasn't I in the other place?

If the bus hadn't been late, I wouldn't have been in that shop then.

If I had picked another checkout to queue at, I would have been quicker.

Why was the bus late?

Why am I where I am at any given moment?

Why did nothing happen? Why did something nearly happen?

And she told me she had got stuck. There were no answers. The questions just kept going round in her head, for ages, even after two more bombs had exploded and the right-wing extremist who had planted them had been imprisoned, and the premiere of a play that had been written about him had been performed.

Annu

Dear Mrs Heiskanen,

I'm writing to let you know that my husband Hamish MacKay died on 23 October. In the end it was fate that won this strange, stupid game.

That stubborn, headstrong man would never put on a life jacket, for all they campaigned here to make us do it. He knew full well how it would end. What he was trying to prove and to whom, God only knows.

I know Hamish liked getting your letters. He was a literary man. I don't know where he got that spark, given his parents were what they were. I suppose that's why he agreed to do the BBC programme – he got to know people who were a bit different. He liked associating with those grand types. I saw it all right.

I wish you luck in your life. Not too much luck, mind.

Hamish was buried in Crossbost churchyard.

Regards,
Mary MacKay

# A MERMAID SPLASHING

# I

The screaming wakes me up. What's the matter with that girl? Why's she making that noise? She's quite normal in the day, but it's like she's possessed at night.

Luckily, Pekka gets up. The bed grows cold when he goes upstairs, though.

If I were here by myself, I wouldn't go and see her, no way. I'd stay safe inside in my own bed and wait for it to end. It would have to end at some point. What a racket.

The stairwell's so cold at night. You're best off not moving until the heat pump comes on again. At night it's like the whole house belongs to someone else: definitely not me, anyway.

There are too many outside doors in this house: one to the front garden and one to the back garden. The cellar and the woodshed have their own doors, too. And you can get in and out through all of them. I want my own way out, a hidey-hole just for me.

It's hard to get a grip on the place. The walls and doors have different tenses – something was there, something isn't there any more, something could be installed there. I hadn't got the hang of those four outside doors until I was awake one night and I started imagining a fire again.

Ever since I was a child, I've imagined fires when I can't get to sleep. I make a mental list of the things I'll take with me and I plan which way I'll run and wonder if the door handles will be too hot to touch by now. The houses, doors and things have changed over the years, but the fire stays the same. My old flat was on the fourth floor and there I often thought of jumping off the balcony. Should I jump, or should I burn? It's hard to know until you're actually in the situation.

Towards the end of September, the nights started getting colder. I asked Pekka to put a proper latch on the cellar door. I had the feeling something was trying to creep in. Chill or damp or a field mouse. I don't want anything to come in through that door apart from home-made apple jam.

And then there are the windows. Once, in summer, I was woken up by a bat flying over the bed! It flew round and round and round, bumping against the lamp every now and then. God! I buried myself under the quilt, head and toes covered, and started shouting. I was yelling in Swedish without even realizing. Pekka took the quilt off me and started massaging my calf, thinking I had cramp again. At last I managed to switch back to Finnish. I'm like, 'Baaaat!' at the top of my voice. Pekka only realized then that there was something fluttering above his head. He got up and the bat came down. I squeezed myself against the bed as flat as I could. I think I screamed.

Pekka swiped at the bat with a scarf and managed to get it to drop down on to the floor. It was hissing and snapping inside the material. It even tried to bite him. In the end Pekka lifted the bundle up towards the window and threw it out.

'Poor thing, it must have been terrified,' Pekka said as he closed the window.

I couldn't believe my ears. He felt sorry for the bat. Somehow, I had behaved childishly, but the poor bat was terrified, landing in this strange place.

The girl's so quiet in the day. I don't know what goes on in her head, and she's not telling. She stares ahead, alone with her thoughts, and just snorts when I try to ask her anything. Nothing really gets a rise out of her.

Sometimes it's sort of creepy, how calmly they sit together. I remember the cleaning day, before the move, when they were shoving things into rubbish bags. Not a word, no crying, either: nothing. They just stuffed the old things into black sacks. They worked in silent agreement. But it made me shiver. The girl was chucking away all the board games, all the soft toys, all the cartoons on DVD, all the old clothes. I tried to say we could take the stuff to the recycling centre but they just wanted to get rid of it all, so we drove to the dump.

I hadn't even been to a dump before. You can't get to one if you don't have a car. I didn't know a dump was like the top of the world. The road winds up a slope. We followed other cars, each carrying a loaded trailer. And at the top, the sky opens. The scenery stretches out in all directions; the motorway roars somewhere below. On top of the mountain of rubbish is a rumbling and rustling, and every so often everything is drowned out by the screech of breaking glass as a whole load of shards gets tipped out on to the ground.

There was a platform at the summit of the tip. Pekka lifted the eight sacks of former life on to that platform. Gulls flew in the sky and a yellow tractor pushed scrap metal into a compact heap with a clanking scoop. All the stuff, all the life, became part of the landscape. It was a land of plastic cobbles. Tractors drove on top of it and clouds of gulls flew overhead. Everything on this mountain is broken, I thought. The sky is open, glass screeches, metal clatters.

And then we drove off with nothing. The wind was fresh, the trailer empty; we glided down the side of the rubbish mountain and back into the world, along with the wind. The girl sat in silence. The motorway flew with us, the wind flew with us, the gulls tried to fly with us but were left helplessly behind. And so we started a new life.


It rustles and crackles here. Detritus falls into the flue and things move inside the walls. Beetles drop off the ceiling. They're big and black and once they've fallen, they lie there, twitching on their backs. When you press your heel on top of them, you hear a dry crunch. What on earth are they doing here?

When the baby is born, I will understand it. I will protect it, run to it when it has a nightmare, and I will no longer fear anything. Splash splash, it flips over. The doctor can say what he likes.

# 2

Pekka says this is a healthy house where all the basics are in order. I'm not quite sure what the basics are. He also says the house hasn't been ruined by makeovers, though from the way he talks I get the impression there was always some building project or other on the go. I could certainly tell there'd been no cleaning done round here for the last three years, because when the evening sun hit the windows, you couldn't see out of them. There were streaks of green pollen all over the glass. And thin spiderwebs everywhere – between the windowpanes, on the light switch, in every corner, and also in funny places like the washbasin, between the toaster and the kitchen roll, all over the rocking chair…The cobwebs were so fine you could only see them because of the dust sticking to the thin threads.

Dead flies on the sills. A buzzing sound somewhere. A wasp flew out of the wood stove. Later that day, I heard the chimney sweep telling Pekka that the easiest way to destroy a wasps' nest was by dropping stones into the chimney. Pekka snapped at him, said we didn't drop anything on top of anyone here. He nearly threw the chimney sweep out there and then.

Pekka was so excited when he brought me to the house for the first time. He told me how he had planned to extend the sauna and build a patio at the edge of the front garden, and he described the kinds of new heating systems we could consider. The yellow wall of the house glowed in the afternoon sun. I thought: three years ago, I couldn't have imagined that I would be standing now in this warmth with a man who wanted to consider heating systems with me.

It's hard to figure the garden out because it's so overgrown. Pekka was talking like there was a lawn, a vegetable patch and a flower bed. But I really couldn't tell at what point the hedge bordering the garden became the forest. Tree seedlings stuck out here and there from the grass at the front. The flower bed was apparently the thing that was buried under a massive rose bush. The string keeping the bush under control had given way, so the rose had fallen forward and started growing along the ground.

A dirty, crooked swing was tangled in a tree; sandpit toys peeped out from among greenery; the berry bushes had been choked by long grass.

But the glass veranda was warm and light. I imagined sitting there in a small, white wicker chair. And I pictured geraniums and stones polished by the sea on the windowsill. And I thought, *this is what makes for happiness*. That there's a veranda, that there's light, that you can dream of wicker chairs.

The hall smelled of a summer cabin or an elderly person's home. The house was older and more wooden than I had imagined, and though it was sunny outside, it was dark indoors. All the inside doors were closed. The varnished wood panelling of the walls reminded me of a ski lodge where we went when I was a child, to drink hot juice.

'This is the kitchen and the living room,' Pekka said, opening the door. He was as excited as a small boy and even his movements were quicker than usual.

I felt a pang, realizing how happy he was, being able to move back home.

It was a real rustic kitchen. It had an old wood stove, a rocking chair and a wall hanging. The floor was covered with long rag rugs. A few children's books lay on the living-room floor, together with a Hungry Hippos game. There was a dirty coffee cup on the windowsill by the sofa. It was as if the room had fallen into an enchanted sleep four years ago. They hadn't even tidied away the unfinished game.

The ceiling light in the kitchen flickered as Pekka connected the fridge-freezer to the wall. The freezer sighed and fizzed but it still started up. And with the sound of the freezer the kitchen came alive. Pekka peered into the fridge, sniffed and shut the door.

When I looked at the kitchen, it hit home for the first time that Pekka was older than me. It didn't matter – it just crossed my mind. Perhaps it was the rag rugs. Or how big the house was. Or the hippo game. The manor house was big, too, but it wasn't his. This was Pekka's home: his hands and steps knew this place; his feet fitted into the boots by the door.

'Well, then,' Pekka said. 'We'd better get started.'

Then he stood in the middle of the kitchen holding a bucket, but he didn't start anything. I didn't know what he wanted to start, exactly, nor if the thing had to do with the bucket, or with me. Maybe the enchanted sleep was still floating about in the room and freezing his brain.

'Is there an upstairs?' I asked.

Pekka swivelled round, came back to life, put the bucket away and rushed to the stairs.


The stairs were made of wood. Each step creaked at a slightly different point and in its own way. The colour of the steps changed from blue to brown after the seventh one, because, according to Pekka, there had previously been a wall and a door at that point. The banister stopped halfway, too. The doorway to the old balcony had been covered by just hardboard, the upstairs landing had no wallpaper, and all four doors leading off it were shut. Varnished a yellowy colour, they looked terribly closed, as if we weren't meant to be there. The backing paper was lumpy, and part of the walls was covered with raw planks. I say 'backing paper', but I don't even know what that is, really.

'This was Saara's room, and the bigger one was ours,' Pekka said, opening the doors.

In the girl's room there was a doll's house and a Winnie-the-Pooh cover on the bed.

'And that door leads to the attic, and here we built a toilet. Otherwise, the upstairs is pretty much in its original state,' Pekka explained. Then he stopped by the door of the bigger bedroom. 'I thought we could have the downstairs bedroom and let Saara have this large one. She'll have her own space that way, a bit of privacy.'

'That'd be fine,' I replied. It *was* fine, too, because I didn't think the upstairs wanted me.

After coming back down, Pekka opened cupboards, fetched a basketful of logs from the woodshed and lit a fire in the stove. I watched him sitting there in front of the stove on a small stool and thought: *this is where he belongs*. He was never a lord of the manor; this, sawdust, is what he knows and understands.

# 3

Pekka was surprised when I suddenly left the antenatal group. I can't explain it to him. I don't need that kind of thing. The baby is growing and moving about; that's enough for now.

'Has it got scales?' the girl asked yesterday.

'Of course not,' I replied. 'It's got skin.'

'Aha,' the girl answered, and carried on with whatever she was doing.

It's got skin and a face and a little snub nose in the middle of its face – you can see it in the ultrasound. It's got hands and fingers and a spine.

'But no legs,' the girl said then.

'Saara…' said Pekka.

'Krista said it herself!' the girl snapped. 'So, has it got legs or not?'

Pekka didn't react, just carried on chopping potatoes. He sank into his own silence, like a diver, blowing bubbles and vanishing into darkness.

'No, as a matter of fact,' I told her. 'You can say it hasn't.'

'There you are, then,' the girl shot back. 'You *can* say: no legs.'

Pekka still doesn't want to talk about it properly. He's angry, though he won't say that out loud. He's angry because I didn't believe the doctor. I tried to, but when I got home, I just didn't any more. I googled the doctor; he was three years younger than me. I missed the second ultrasound and then within a week, the whole thing had just kind of disappeared. I started the antenatal group and was like all the other mothers there. Pekka and I went out and got a cot. I bought a liner for it decorated with seahorses and fish.

My bump floats in the silence. Or rather, my bump is the silence. Even though I pull my coat round my belly so the seams are really straining, no sound comes out. That's where the diver sinks. There are tubes, oxygen and darkness down there.

When Pekka rests his ear against my watery belly, listening, everything's OK. The baby splashes. This is just how I imagined it. Pekka said himself you always love your child, whatever it's like. You don't need to go on a course to learn that.

Anyway, miracles do happen. I'm the first to believe in miracles.

# 4

The girl's shouting again. It's night, and the room is pitch-black. I hear Pekka grabbing something from the chair to put on and charging upstairs. I can hear what they're saying through the ceiling.

The girl: 'No no no…Don't look!'

Pekka: 'Saara, open your eyes.'

The girl: 'They are open!'

Pekka: 'Come on, open your eyes.'

The girl: 'They are open.'

Pekka: 'No, they're not. Saara, open your eyes.'

The bed clatters as the girl kicks and thrashes her adolescent arms and legs about. I've told Pekka she needs a new bed; she'll be taller than I am soon. A bed with no sides, so we don't have to listen to that clattering. She can fall on the floor for all I care.

At last it all goes quiet. I can hear Pekka moving and the floor creaking. The girl must have fallen asleep.

Ten minutes pass. Pekka's still not back. No creaking, no more shouting, nothing. Somewhere in the distance, the brakes of trucks squeal; they sound so alive at night. Sometimes I'm not sure if it's a dog or a truck or an unhappy person. Boohooooo.

The house is cold.

The upstairs has swallowed Pekka.

Boohooooo.

I sit in bed and wait for a bit.

Finally, I switch on the bedside lamp and get up. I put on a jumper and slippers and walk into the hall. That's weird, too, that we never just wear socks indoors here. There are shoes scattered all over the hall floor. I stumble over one of Pekka's boots. I'd like to switch on the heat pump. The pump and I, we belong to the same world, where there's light, heat and humming. When I come home, I always press the button straight away and the pump welcomes me. It's like a homecoming button. The pump beeps and opens up its flaps for me. The home gets going, humming and warming up.

'Pekka,' I call out into the stairwell, but there's no reply.

I climb the creaking stairs that change colour halfway up. The varnished doors of the upstairs landing are shut. They're always shut; gravity and the wonky house make them close by themselves. A thin strip of light shines out from the girl's room.

Pekka is asleep on the edge of the girl's bed. He's curled up uncomfortably against the wooden side, using his elbow as his pillow, his knees sticking out over the edge. His skin is covered with goose pimples. There he sleeps, a big man without a quilt, on the edge of a red child's bed all covered with stickers.

And behind Pekka's back sleeps the girl. She snuffles lightly like a small animal, her face relaxed and ageless. Sometimes people look like babies when they're asleep, sometimes they appear older and wiser than they are, but the girl seems to combine all ages at the same time.

With her eyes closed and lips slightly parted, she actually looks quite beautiful. By day, she frowns and purses her lips so much that it's hard even to see her features. Somehow, she lacks joy. I do understand it. Right now, watching her sleep, I see that she simply lacks joy.

How on earth do they fit in one bed? I suppose it's something parents and children can do and others find hard to understand. They find peace in each other, even in awkward positions. There's a kind of magic to it. The parent's strength grows with the child's weight; they say that even when a woman has had a caesarean, she can lift her baby and the wound can take it. Once in the library I saw a father carrying his disabled son. The boy was school age but not able to stand, even with support. They'd left the wheelchair at the bottom of the steps. The father carried the boy with ease, as if his son were a baby, as if he hadn't even noticed that his son had grown. I watched the father as he climbed the steps, the boy in his arms, and wondered if that father's strength would last to the end. Would his strength grow, as after a caesarean, so he'd be able to carry his son even when the boy was an adult?

The bodies of Pekka and the girl curve in the same way. Their eyes form the same lines. I hadn't noticed before how similar they look.

In the morning, we both sit at the table, the girl and me. It seems we're as tired as each other. We listen to the crackling of the breakfast cereal in her bowl. Ever since she had braces put in, she hasn't eaten bread. That was a right hooha. Amazing how helpless a grown man can look under pressure from a small, frowning girl and a couple of metal wires. 'I won't have them,' the girl announced, pinching her lips together. Pekka sweated and pleaded. He went online and dug out a list of famous people who had had braces. But then, luckily for all of us, the girl got a dentist who was young and funny and also into mountain climbing. She was so impressed that the braces were no longer a problem.

'I have a recurring nightmare, too,' I say as I'm refilling the coffee cups.

'Oh. What happens in it?'

'I'm at a party and I shoot everyone there. Pekka, you, my brother and sister, my mum, everyone.'

The girl replies: 'Oh.'

It feels like she's looking at me properly for the first time.

After a moment, she asks, 'D'you know how to shoot in real life?'

'No. Only when I'm dreaming.'

Why am I telling her this? Do I want to get into a bed of nightmares with them, to share whatever it is they've got? Do I want a black bin bag of my own, which I can stuff with things? Without any questions, without any explanations?

'Do you know what the wishbone of a chicken is?' the girl asks then.

'The one you pull with your little fingers?'

'Yeah,' the girl replies, stirring her cereal. 'I heard the click in my dream. But then the bone was a key but I lost it. And I had to cut off my little finger with scissors so it could be a key.'

'Lucky it was just a dream,' I said.

'No, it's from Grimm's fairy tales.'

'There's one like that?'

When I changed the girl's sheets over the weekend, I found a huge pair of golden scissors under her pillow. They were probably her mother's: they're like the ones used to cut velvet in fabric shops. I didn't feel like asking about them; I just put them in the desk drawer.

# 5

The cold slinks about on the floor and makes my ankles hurt. Somehow, in this house, the border between outside and inside is not as clear as in a block of flats. The weather comes in, the mud comes in, the wind comes in, creepy-crawlies and bats come in. We haven't got a doorbell, either. Or we do, but it doesn't work. Here, people just stroll into the hall. But Pekka keeps a close eye on the interior doors; you've got to shut all doors after you or he gets uptight. One day he explained that the brickwork at the centre of the house is like a warm heart jointly heated by separate fireboxes. And I thought: the centre of this house is an ice-cold hall, more like. We heat the rooms on the edges and keep the cold out with these thin interior doors, but in the hall, a chilly draught blows.

Yesterday I was at home on my own and it got so cold I decided to light a fire in the stove. Pekka had shown me the dampers and the hatches but I couldn't remember which damper was for what, so I opened all of them to be on the safe side. I lit the fire and thought about how cosy it looks when you're arriving home and there's smoke coming out of the chimney.

There was smoke all right, but it didn't go up into the chimney. First it came curling out from the edges of the stove plates, then from all sides of the stove. All of a sudden, the whole kitchen was full of smoke. I opened and shut the hatch, added fuel to the fire, opened the dampers wider – nothing helped. How on earth could I put the fire out? Should I throw water on it? I pulled the charred logs out and a whole load of ash spilled out with them. Smoke poured out of the hatch into the room and pushed its way through every joint of the stove. Quite a lot of joints, a stove has.

The chimney had to be blocked. What could have dropped into it? What if the chimney caught fire, if there was a dead gull in there? My eyes were stinging because I'd been running around in the smoke; my hair and everything else stank of it. I knocked my head on the brick dome of the stove and I was too embarrassed to call Pekka.

By the time he finally got home, I had managed to get rid of some of the smoke. I had opened all the doors and the room temperature was down to sixteen. I was lying in the bedroom; there's an electric heater in there.

That evening, Pekka showed me a circular hatch on the side of the wood stove. When you open it, you find an empty tuna-fish tin in the flue. You pour a drop of lighter fuel in and leave it burning in the flue for a quarter of an hour. Then the chimney warms up and starts drawing.

Today, as I was going through the washing, I found three pairs of bloodstained knickers in the laundry basket. The small scrunched-up bundles had been pushed right to the bottom.

I went to the bathroom, where Pekka and the girl were brushing their teeth. I don't know why they always do that at the same time, but that's the habit they've got into. Neither of them locks the toilet door – they walk in just like that even though someone else might be in there already. Sometimes the girl comes in to brush her teeth while I'm in the middle of doing a wee. Sometimes all three of us have our morning wash at the same time. 'Not enough room in here,' says the girl. I've half a mind to say, 'It's not really meant to hold a crowd.' Sometimes I lock the door but that seems to blow their minds. They're all like rattling the handle and asking if you're doing a poo! They can't seem to get it into their heads that you might just want to wash your face in peace.

'Have you started your periods?' I ask.

'S'pose,' the girl answers through toothpaste.

Pekka looks at the girl and then at me, and finally at the scrunched-up knickers in my hand. He's got a surprised expression on his face.

The girl spits and gargles.

'Your daughter has started her periods,' I say to Pekka. And then, all of a sudden, I feel like crying. I don't know where that's come from; I just carry on clutching the knickers.

Pekka stands there with the towel against his cheek, glancing at both of us in turn. Clearly, he doesn't know what to do.

'Why didn't you say anything?' he asks the girl then.

'I don't know,' she answers.

'Surely you could have told us,' I say.

I feel so sad. Doesn't she dare talk to us? Doesn't she like being here? Does she miss her mum? How can I breathe some life into her?

'You can talk to us about anything,' I say, and again I feel like crying. Who am I to tell anyone what they should or shouldn't talk about? I'm ashamed. I don't even glance at Pekka. Please, someone, say that to me. *Go on, tell me everything, you can tell me everything.*

'Get dressed and we'll go shopping,' I say to the girl. Then I hand Pekka the washing.

'Put them to soak, will you. Do you remember what towels Hannele used?'

'Why?'

'I don't know, I just thought…I don't want to intrude…'

'Are you saying there's something…hereditary about it?'

'No, no,' I answer.

Pekka looks at the shelf. Then he shakes his head. 'They went to the dump. It might have been a purple pack?'

The girl and I get ready to go. She agrees to come with me and even allows me a little hug. She ties my shoelaces because I can't reach them myself any more.

Pekka stays behind in the bathroom to do the laundry. I look at his back as he stands in front of the washbasin.

# 6

'Good-bye, feet! Oh, my poor little feet, I wonder who will put on your shoes and stockings for you now, dears? I'm sure I shan't be able! I shall be a great deal too far off to trouble myself about you: you must manage the best way you can.'

In the last few days, I've been thinking back to *Alice in Wonderland*, a book we had on the shelf when I was a child. In the story, Alice went into the Rabbit's house to fetch his fan and white gloves, but while inside, Alice got it into her head to drink from a bottle she found on the table. Then she began to grow. In the end she grew so big that she got stuck inside the house. The Rabbit raged outside and threatened to set the house on fire.

In the book's black-and-white illustrations, Alice was ugly, with a big head. She wore children's clothes but her face looked adult. And when she spoke, I felt like covering my ears or shutting my eyes because she drifted from one thing to another at random and annoyed everyone. Something about those pictures frightened me and made me feel sick, but I still kept looking at them.

There's one that sticks in my mind: Alice's neck stretched like a turkey's. She was like a plasticine creature who has been grabbed by the head and ankles and stretched out. Only, she wasn't made of plasticine but muscle and bone. A gigantic, slithery thing with a horrified expression on her face. Her hair stood on end; the collar of her blouse was straining. Why was it so repulsive that someone's body was different from your own? My own neck tingled and bile rose to my throat. I felt in my own spine how Alice's vertebrae tightened and her skin stretched.

'Stupid girl! Get out, straight away, or I'll set the house on fire!' the Rabbit was shouting outside his house. By now, Alice had expanded to fill the living room. A gigantic child's arm stuck out of one downstairs window. From another there was a leg sticking out, covered by a knee-high sock. The Rabbit was throwing kindling into the house.

Such a nasty, foolish animal. Can't people be whatever size or shape they want to be? I thought of the doctor examining the ultrasound image. What right did he have to stand there and throw kindling as if you could just undo a baby just like that? What could I do about it not being the 'right' size and appearance?

Everybody was nasty to Alice the whole time. It wasn't her fault that she had grown so fast and got stuck. She only went in because she wanted to help.

Maybe we all end up in places where we're too big and can't move at some point. And not all of us will have pieces of cake in our pocket so we can shrink to the size the doctor says is OK.

# 7

'Look what we've got!' Pekka says, still with his coat on. He starts piling parcels on to the kitchen table, different sizes, all wrapped in bloody paper. There's a strong smell in the air.

The girl and I move closer.

'It doesn't get fresher than this, I tell you. Can't get this down the shop. This is ethical and organic and locally sourced and damn good.' Pekka starts opening the parcels, all enthusiastic.

The mutton is dark and thick and the sheep smell of it is really pungent. Bones stick out here and there. Shoulder, kneecap, ribs.

'Annu's decided to spend the spring in Scotland. Don't ask me why. She's had the sheep slaughtered. A friend of hers is driving around the whole province at the moment, distributing meat to people Annu knows.'

'I thought we were going to have the sheep here, in our garden,' the girl says from the doorway, to where she's retreated, having seen the parcels.

'What do you mean, here? We don't even have a decent fence,' Pekka replies. He doesn't register the girl's expression.

'What have we got here?' I ask.

'A whole sheep,' Pekka answers.

'Which sheep?' the girl asks, but Pekka doesn't respond.

He's opened all the parcels and the table's covered with meat. He puts the pieces in order: neck, ribs, shoulder, roasting meat, sirloin, tenderloin, shanks. Mince he places in the middle, as if forming a stomach. There it is: a sheep cut to pieces.

'We were supposed to get Bruno!' the girl shouts. She bursts into tears and stomps upstairs.

'Well, we didn't really…' Pekka starts. He stops because the girl has already disappeared. 'Oh dear.'


Pekka fetches a carving knife and a chopping board. He marches between table and cupboards as if excited by the smell of the blood and the meat.

'We should really chop them into smaller pieces before they go in the freezer,' he declares, handing me the kitchen scissors. 'You could take off the membranes; this one hasn't been trimmed terribly well, from the look of it.'

Then he pushes a lump of meat towards me. It's still got blood in the creases. The membrane shines, rainbow-coloured.

Pekka's knife grinds into bone as I cut. The smell of bloody meat fills the kitchen.

I try not to think about muscles and the order all these pieces were in under the skin. I cut into the red meat and try not to think of the small, splashing creature who lacks a kidney and a rectum and God knows what else. I try not to think about how it's been put together: what sort of lumps and the order they're in. I think of rosemary, garlic, salt and potatoes. I think of a chicken. It's white and slimy and doesn't smell.

When I was little, my favourite parts of the chicken were the cheeks. The two soft pieces of meat at the bottom of the chicken were what I called 'cheeks'. Dad took them off for me with his fingers; they plopped out of their sockets like eyes and they were deliciously tender as they'd been simmering in the juice of the meat. I don't know what part of the chicken the cheeks actually were. They weren't cheeks, of course, because the whole head was missing. I expect they were in the chicken's back, near the tail or the neck; I don't know which. Maybe they were the flight muscles.

Everything's all mixed up, topsy-turvy. I bump into door frames, I shove kindling into the wrong holes and even my own shoelaces disappear from view. I looked up images of embryos on the internet. The worst were like chickens. There was nothing identifiable about them, whichever way you looked at them, from the top or bottom.

The girl doesn't come down to eat in the evening. She sulks in her room, refusing to answer when Pekka goes to the door to talk to her.

# 8

The girl was at school and Pekka at work. I started watching the execution of American aid workers on the internet. On the news, they only show the initial image and then say the rest has been cut. I suppose I just wanted to see what it looked like.

Of course, I should have realized that when a clip lasts for three minutes and sixteen seconds, it's not going to be instant. They call it 'beheading' so I was thinking of those films where the axe swings once and the head falls. I went on clicking and clicking and just couldn't stop. The clips had captions in Arabic and also Spanish because some of the material belonged to Mexican drug gangs. There were knives, swords and chainsaws. There were orange overalls and heads dangling by the hair. There were family men and black flags. There were bones, tendons and T-shirts. God help us, there was music.

Luckily Pekka is the first to come home.

The baby splashes about, kicking vigorously; maybe the videos upset it, too.

Pekka: 'What's going on here?'

Me: 'A man's head was being cut off.'

Pekka: 'Where? What with?'

Me: 'On the computer. With a knife.'

Pekka: 'What is this about, Krista…?'

Me: 'It wasn't a quick job, either. And another man was on his knees next to him, waiting for his turn.'

Pekka: 'What made you go and watch something like that?'

Me: 'Three minutes sixteen seconds.'

Pekka: 'Come on, darling…'

I've got to go to the toilet and throw up. When I come back to the kitchen, Pekka has switched off the computer. He looks at me from the other side of the room. He looks me in the eye. He takes hold of my face and looks. I struggle to make my eyes stop moving. My head swings as if it couldn't stay still. Stop, I tell my head, don't disappear. Don't roll down, head.

'It's so terrible…' I begin.

'Hush,' Pekka says.

'Why did I go and watch something like that?'

'Hush.'


In bed, I lie in Pekka's arms for a bit. We do that every night. Pekka fiddles with my hair and my hand rests on his chest.

'We once had a visit from a policeman at the manor,' Pekka says softly. 'He came in civilian clothing but he showed me his identity card when he introduced himself. He was one of the ones who were here when Hannele died. He said he was very sorry, and he'd leave straight away if I wanted him to. He asked to see a photo of Hannele.'

Pekka sighs.

'He was having nightmares. And he thought he might feel better if he knew what Hannele had looked like when she was alive. There we sat on the sofa, the constable and me, looking at photos. I showed him the album with the pictures of our summer in Lapland and some photos taken at home here. Renovation stuff, things like that. The constable lived in a similar sort of place, so we had a long chat about loft insulation and the best way to divide the upstairs into three rooms. He had an interesting idea about it and he drew me a plan in a notebook. Then finally he said thank you, stood up and went. And he never came back, so perhaps the photos did help.'

Pekka stares up at the ceiling. He's got an intense look of concentration on his face. As if a big plaster were being removed from a hairy spot.

During the night, I'm woken up by a distant shout. This time, it doesn't come from upstairs, but from inside my head. The voice shouts, 'Off with her head! Off with her head! I'll behead each one of you!'

And then someone swings a flamingo whose beak has been taped shut. The bird's skull knocks against a croquet ball.

'How can you cut off a head when the body's missing?' asks the Cheshire Cat, whose head floats down on to the croquet field.

'Of course you can. You have a neck! And if you have a neck, it can be cut!' the Queen shouts. 'Execute that cat and if my command is not obeyed immediately, I sentence everyone present to headlessness!'

A flamingo is pushed into my arms. I try to take hold of its body but its legs are sticking out all over the place, its feathers are flying about and its neck is all limp. I don't want to hit the ball. The bird, silenced by the tape, stares at me upside down.

'Are you going to hit it, or shall I?' the Queen shouts. And without waiting for an answer, she hits.


Pekka is asleep.

I wish I could go somewhere, ring someone's doorbell, ask to look at photos.

# 9

I go for a walk after the check-up. The health centre is next to a forest with a running track. At this time of day, I can waddle in peace: the track is empty of joggers, or dogs, or ponies from the riding stables.

I went to the antenatal group three times. We talked about our expectations of giving birth, compared baby equipment, discussed breastfeeding. All the women were nice, and we all had bumps of about the same size.

I don't know why I had to tell them. I hadn't even plucked up the courage to tell Pekka at that point, although I knew I should have. But as everyone shared their own feelings about pregnancy and motherhood, it suddenly seemed possible. As if something in me had waited for a moment when it was all right to say it, and then it came.

And so on the third occasion I said that our baby's limbs had grown together like a tail and it wasn't certain how long it would live. I listed the body parts and organs it lacked.

The other mothers asked how I dared to give birth to a child like that. The mothers asked if we hadn't had a nuchal translucency scan performed. They said I was really strong and they probably wouldn't be able to do what I was doing. But I realized they pitied me. Suddenly, the other mothers didn't want to hear about what kind of baby carrier I was thinking of getting and what I thought of co-sleeping. Suddenly, they were all at pains to make clear that their situations and their babies were totally different from mine. Their babies were normal and ours wasn't. One woman started crying because she thought the death of a baby was such a terrible thing. Really, you shouldn't even talk about it, in case you catch the bad luck.

'Our baby isn't dead,' I would have liked to say. 'It hasn't been born yet. And not all of them die.' I didn't say how many didn't, but they didn't ask, either. No one wanted to look at the ultrasound picture and admire the button-nosed sweetie. And when it was time to choose a partner for neck massage, the woman who had said you mustn't talk about the death of a baby suddenly turned away, as if death could spread from my neck to her hands.


Late autumn is so quiet. The birds, the flies and the leaves have gone. There's not a sound. Over there I can see a chanterelle poking out, but I leave it – I can't be bothered to stuff it into my handbag.

Is there no one here?

The ancient Greeks used to lower the gods on to the stage when the plot of a play got into a knot and the characters weren't able to work it out themselves. Gods in white clothing in their little box, descending creakily to the middle of the stage with the help of a rope. There they could declare judgement. It wasn't thought to be quite as skilful an ending as one where the characters solved their problems themselves, but it was better than nothing.

I walk a kilometre. Then, without warning, a rushing begins. A wave rising, rising in the middle of this silent forest, and suddenly I'm invaded by the feeling that everything is crumbling. I won't stay in one piece; I'll trickle into this shrubbery and all that will remain is a wet patch. Now I make a sound; I pant in the forest. What does that sound like? I find it hard to grasp. How come I'm here, all alone? Help. Help me. I stand there – no, here – in the middle of a sawdust path, and I can't even take hold of a pine trunk. I stand here – it is here, I'm so totally here – and I don't know what will happen now. I'm totally here, because there may not be anything else.

Everything is crumbling.

I hold so much water, an entire ocean. The sharp rocks on the shore stab my sides. Sometimes a whole cliff will crumble into the ocean and people will come rushing with their buckets to dig for fossils.

I'm so totally here; everything else has gone.

How can one baby need so many litres? Salt water pushes through my skin and rises to my lungs in waves. A sea creature kicks inside me. The rushing is so loud. Lower the gods! I try to carry on walking but the water rises up from my stomach. I stop by the exercise equipment to gasp for oxygen. Maybe my womb has torn and the water has flowed into my whole body. I press my hand against my mouth to prevent the ocean from coming out.

The baby must have water.

Water's good.

Luckily, I don't feel any pain.

That must be a good thing: there's no pain.

Is it me standing here? Is that my panting I hear, here, next to the gym equipment? Please help that woman now, gods; have mercy on her. How come I'm so alone? Couldn't someone run past, at least? Come and cuddle me, here by the chanterelle.

The water ebbs. No, this isn't happening. So that's how it is. The water ebbs and my skin holds out. This isn't happening.

This is not my life. Walk. I carry on walking.

# AND THAT WAS THE
# END OF THAT

# I

Once upon a time, there was a father who went hiking in Lapland. He hiked all alone, even though it was dangerous, because you can break your leg in the forest and then you're in trouble.

On the third day, Father heard tinkling in the forest. He didn't know if it was morning or evening; his watch was in town and the sun shone day and night. But he heard the sound and then spotted Mother between the trees. She was walking with a bell tied to her rucksack; it chimed to repel bears. Mother had come to Lapland on her own, too. She was soaking wet, because she had just waded through a wide river to get to the shop more quickly. Crossing the river shortened Mother's trek to the shop, which sold chocolate, by two days. Father found the wet Mother enchanting, and he shared his remaining chocolate with her. He had five pieces left, and Mother received three of them (an important point).

Father and Mother found themselves in love, and away they walked from the fell.

Mother lived in a small village at the edge of a big forest with her three aunts, whom she called Auntie Brown, Auntie Marshmallow and Auntie Uncle.

The small village comprised only five houses. The forest, in contrast, was so large that you could walk through it to the Soviet Union and Lapland.

When Mother got home, Auntie Brown, Auntie Marshmallow and Auntie Uncle were terribly cross because Mother had gone to Lapland on her own in secret. It didn't make any difference that Mother had taken a bear bell with her. Then the aunts got angry because Mother had come back from Lapland with the bearded Father. No one quite knew exactly why Mother, an educated person with a degree, lived with three aunts in the middle of nowhere. But Mother brought Father into the house of the three aunts, who sniffed in a dissatisfied way. To everyone's surprise, the aunts took to Father and fed him cake and casserole. The following summer, Father repaired the sauna roof and the aunts forgave him everything. Then Mother and Father got married, had the Lovely Baby and moved to Sawdust House. And that was the end of that.

Mum and Dad had their own versions of the summer they met in Lapland. I liked them both. But perhaps I liked Dad's version more because the mother tinkling like a bear bell sounded like a character from a fairy tale. I also liked the way Dad mimicked the dissatisfied aunts, who ended up cooking him casserole and calling him 'our Pekka'.

Mum's version concentrated on the three aunts. I was afraid of them because they sounded so strict and the surrounding forest was so big.

Mum was better at describing the Lovely Baby. Dad really wallowed in the way the doctor cut Mum's tummy open and Dad nearly fainted, while Mum's version concentrated on me alone. I was pale and beautiful, with large, round eyes and an orange snub nose. A woman in a cafe asked if the baby had a battery inside – it was as sweet as a doll!

The three aunts were real, but two of them died while I was still the Lovely Baby. Auntie Marshmallow was alive and in a care home. Sometimes I went with Mum to visit her there. Auntie Marshmallow lay in bed and Mum told her about the garden and the vegetable patch, and asked for advice about how to look after some of the plants, though she never followed it.

In the end it turned out that Auntie Marshmallow lived longer than Mum. She was brought to the funeral in a wheelchair. She sat there with a confused expression on her face, as if she didn't understand what was going on. Her skin looked as thin as tissue paper. The floral wreath trembled in her hands, and eventually, someone picked it up from her lap and placed it on Mum's coffin. That's when Auntie Marshmallow became agitated and her wheelchair was pushed away.

That wasn't the last time I saw Auntie Marshmallow; I went to see her again with Dad. We were living at the manor house then, but because Dad didn't want to talk about Mum and wasn't able to talk about the vegetable patch, we didn't go again.

After Mum's death, Dad's story became crushed ice. Once, he tried to tell it, but when he got to the part where Mum crosses the river, he stopped.

Mum was interrupted, and we couldn't tell the end of her story. Mum was a character in a fairy tale who rose from a river and wandered through dark, gloomy forests to the Soviet Union and Lapland and back. And if characters like that die, they don't die in vain, and stupidly. They don't abandon the Lovely Baby, whose clothes they warm in front of the fire; at least, they don't go away without leaving a message. I waited for a message for a long time. I read books and thought that one day, a letter would fall out of one of them and everything would be resolved. Or perhaps Mum would have underlined some sentences and all I had to do was find the right book. And I thought about time and the fact that in those underlined words, Mum would be here and now, even if it were only one more time.

Auntie Marshmallow remained in the care home. The Lovely Baby was covered by a wall panel and we moved to Extra Great Manor.

It was a bad ending, but it was the best we could do.

## 2

The end of the world would be good, maybe. Everything would end at once, and it would be clear. The dinosaurs died because a meteorite collided with the Earth and everything went dark with ash. I like that image. A thick carpet of ash falls softly over the globe like Auntie Annu's wool, and everyone dies. At some point, later, when the soil is being dug up, the thick, grey carpet will be found inside the earth. It will be everywhere, evenly, in every country. And inside, asleep, will be dinosaurs, animals, trees and all the grassy fields of the Earth.

If the end of the world doesn't work out, there's always an alternative: Paradise. Auntie Annu said she heard Paradise will only come if all the people in the world are without sin for one moment. One moment would be enough, but it would have to be the same moment for everyone. A world without sin for one small, shared moment, and Paradise will pop out. A trumpet will sound, angels will swoosh and the world will end.

I'm not sure about Paradise. I don't trust angels.

Sometimes, in the manor house, I used to lie in my metal bed and imagine ways of getting Paradise started. If everyone could be made to sleep at the same time, it might work, because you can't sin when you're asleep, even if you're having a nightmare.

Or maybe it could be announced on TV, on the news, and in the papers: tomorrow at eight o'clock everyone has to be absolutely still for one minute and not do or think anything bad. I wondered how the information could be got to every person, even those who didn't watch TV or read the papers. If you started spreading the word early enough, would absolutely everyone get to hear about it? What about people living in a jungle or criminals in prison or people whose language no one else spoke? What if someone didn't want to be without sin at that very moment? Could you force them? Those were the sorts of things I was thinking until my grey cells got all knotted up and I fell asleep.

If there's no ending, there's no story. Jesus knew that when he organized Easter. That's why you can't bypass the end of the world. And that's precisely why the ministers at the Easter service got on my nerves when I was little: they really knew how to ruin a good story.

Maybe not everyone wants Paradise. Maybe most people don't want any kind of ending because they're afraid of death. And that's why Paradise doesn't come, and things just happen.

And perhaps, after all, that's why the world goes on: because things happen. Overlapping, at the wrong time, at different times, in the wrong places. If everything were in order, as the angels command, if the angels said 'don't look', and everyone obeyed, we would end up in Paradise with one blast of the trumpet. But the world goes on and life happens, because there's always a person who peeks all the same. Someone forgets to watch the news, someone starts a quarrel when they shouldn't, someone else just doesn't feel like being good, and someone happens to be standing at the edge of the garden when a lump of ice falls. And that's why we'll never reach Paradise.

# 3

Krista is asleep on the sofa. Her trouser buttons are undone and her shirt is rolled up; her big, bare bump lies there in the middle. Blue veins pass under her skin like cables in a wall. Her belly button sticks up. Maybe it's a button for lighting up an aquarium. The skin is so thin and so tautly stretched that if there were a lamp inside her belly, you'd be sure to see through it. Dark shapes float inside, in the cloudy water among the veins: liver, spleen, Krista's guts and an embryo.

Krista sleeps but her belly doesn't. According to the doctor, it's a miracle that the embryo is alive. I think it's miraculous how the whole, gigantic, white belly flops from left to right. And then does it again. There's a mermaid inside Krista, I've heard Dad say so. Krista's belly holds a half fish but it hasn't got scales or legs. And we're not allowed to talk about it.

Sometimes Krista rocks on top of a gym ball, sighing. She lets out sounds and gets into positions that make me feel embarrassed. She goes on all fours in the middle of the living room with her watery belly hanging like a sack between her legs and her arms. She lotions her stomach and picks off the hairs that have suddenly sprouted above her belly button. Sometimes she can't reach them and Dad has to pull them out with tweezers. She does breathing exercises that make all the mounds of her body rise, and occasionally a fart comes out.

One day, a friend comes to visit Krista, and they sit in the armchairs in the living room, drinking tea and chatting. They're talking about something to do with breasts; her friend's pregnant, too. Then Krista suddenly says, 'Can I show you?' She undoes her shirt and takes out her breast. She squeezes her nipple and says, 'Isn't that crazy?' Then they both laugh, because a drop of sticky milk has come out of Krista's nipple even though no baby's been born yet.

My breasts are still small. I put sports tape on the nipples so they don't stick out through my T-shirt. If you use the tape too often, though, you get a rash.


After her friend's gone, Krista asks me to chop up salad ingredients with her. She always wants us to prepare food together, but she has these strict rules.

I hope she won't undo her shirt buttons for me. To be on the safe side, I decide to tell her a story.

'Once upon a time, a sheep gave birth at the manor house,' I begin. I don't let on immediately what kind of story's going to follow.

'Really?' Krista asks, snipping a cucumber into slices with a knife. Her slices are thick, and she cuts them by holding the cucumber diagonally. She thinks that gives the best result.

'One evening, a leg and half a head were hanging out of one of the sheep's bums.'

Krista laughs.

'Auntie Annu tried to help and gave it a bit of a pull. But the lamb had got stuck. Its leg was folded and its elbow was bent and it didn't have enough room to get out.'

'Did you call a vet?'

'No, Annu fetched Dad. Then they tried to pull together. Annu held the lamb like this, Dad was pulling the lamb out, and every time he tugged, the sheep cried like this: Baa! Baa!'

'And Dad let you watch?'

'It was a bit like a toy with a string you pull. Baa! Baa!'

'That's bad.'

Krista tips the thick, slanting slices into a bowl. Then she takes an avocado, cuts it in half and opens it up. She smacks the seed hard with a knife and turns the avocado over.

'The tugging took so long that it got quite dark. I held the torch and lit the sheep's bum up. In the end, Annu phoned some man, who explained how the lamb had to be pushed back and turned round into a better position. Guess what, Annu's hand went into the sheep this deep!'

I stretch out my arm and point to my elbow.

'Then Auntie Annu began shouting like this: "Ouuuuch!" Dad and I got frightened 'cause we didn't know what was going on.'

Krista stares at me and my arm.

'Are you having me on?' she asks, looking unsure.

'No. The sheep's bum closed up and Annu's arm got stuck inside.'

'Like a contraction?'

'Yes. They say it hurts a lot. Then, when it was over, Auntie got her arm out. And then the lamb's leg went into the right position and it was born. It was really slimy.'

'Wow,' Krista says, going to wash her hands. 'Pekka's never said anything about that.'

'If your baby gets stuck, maybe they'll do the same to you.'

'Hardly.'

'The next morning the lamb was dead. Even though Auntie took it to a warm place and made it sneeze like you're supposed to. It still died.'

'Listen, I'm going to go and rest for a bit,' Krista says, leaving the kitchen.

I don't even have time to say that the story isn't finished yet.


Dad and Auntie Annu drank brandy after the lamb had been born. Dad sent me to fetch the coat he had left in the meadow. I took a torch along with me.

Tree branches always look so strange when you shine a torch on them. As if they were being X-rayed. Black became white, and surprising things became visible. My own light-blue coat shone brightly. I hoped a bat wouldn't bump into me.

The sheep dozed in the grass; they were faint, faded blotches in the middle of the dark garden. They were behaving as if nothing had happened. The lamb and its mother had been carried to the warm barn.

Just as I saw Dad's coat, in the sheep pen, the torchlight glinted at the edge of the enclosure.

A fox was standing there. Its eyes lit up like two round lamps as the light hit them. I stood still. The fox stiffened a little but didn't stop eating. Its mouth was wet. What was it eating?

I walked closer and picked up Dad's coat. There was a heap of shiny, blood-drenched pulp lying between the fox's feet. I realized it was the placenta from the birth of the lamb.

When I stood up again, the fox gulped audibly. Then it snatched up the leftover placenta in its mouth and slunk away into the darkness.

# 4

Once I saw a programme about an Indian girl who had never seen a man or a boy naked, not even without a shirt. When the girl's breasts began to grow, she imagined that the man's chest had two hollows into which the woman's breasts would sink. That was the way a man and a woman fitted together. She thought so up until the day of her wedding.

I liked the Indian girl and how little she knew. I imagined Indian breasts pressing into male, Indian holes, two hearts beating close to each other and warmth spreading into every nook and cranny.

# 5

I wake up, hearing a noise coming from the direction of the chest of drawers.

Grating, crunching, then the occasional metallic click. I can't see the chest of drawers; the whole room is too dark. I'm too scared to put the light on; I just lie still under the cover and listen.

It's the sound of scissors. Somebody is using scissors in a dark corner of my room. They're cutting slowly, as if the scissors were blunt or the material too thick. I can't see anything but I can hear the scissors clearly. First a click, then crunch, crunch, crunch. The scissors are labouring away; the darkness persists.

Suddenly, I see a grey line. It runs from top to bottom in the middle of the blackness in the corner. And as the scissors cut, the grey line gets longer. Someone's cutting a hole in the dark. The darkness is black but it's backed with grey. The line curves and finally acquires a shape. It isn't a door; it's a tall, slim figure cutting itself out. It *is* the hole. The hole has detached itself from the dark and is now starting to move.

Terror strikes my chest. I gasp for air. There is not the slightest sound. Blood throbs in my ears; all I hear is the hammering of my own blood.

In books, ghosts are white, but this ghost is black. Sheer, cut-out darkness. And as it walks, the darkness closes up behind it.

It's holding a pair of scissors and it looks like Mum. As soon as I recognize Mum, I stop trying to shout. It's Mum. After all these years, Mum has come back as a ghost.

The ghost has got Mum's hair and Mum's tall body. It's got its head intact. Its fingers are bony and the smoking hand is raised in that familiar way, though it isn't holding a cigarette right now but a pair of scissors. Its knee clicks in a familiar way. It's Mum, only it's empty. It's Mum who's been taken away, a hole left by Mum in my bedroom.

The ghost walks to the end of my bed, and my toes feel chilly. As if the dark were sucking me towards my toes, as if my toes were going to break off soon. And perhaps they will, because now the ghost is raising its scissors. They're the downstairs nail scissors, which I use to cut my toenails, only now they've grown to the size of kitchen scissors. I start kicking the quilt and shouting. And suddenly my lungs pop open, like a bottle, and my voice comes back. The darkness sparkles and I'm a kicking, screaming mess of blanket.

'Saara, Saara, Saara.' Dad repeats my name as he strides up the stairs.

'Stop kicking. Open your eyes.'

'My eyes are open!' I shout with my eyes shut.

'You must have had a nightmare,' Dad says soothingly. He strokes the blanket on top of my head.

I daren't open my eyes.

'What kind of dream were you having?' Dad asks.

I shake my head firmly. Then Dad just sits on the edge of my bed and lets me be. In the end, I come out from under the cover, my hair and neck wet with sweat.

'You've got growing pains,' Dad mutters. He pushes sweaty strands of hair off my face. These days, that's Dad's standard explanation for everything. Dad can't believe some of Mum's old clothes already fit me. He thinks growing up that fast must hurt.


After Dad's gone, I lie in bed quietly, thinking. The Lovely Baby lies there wondering why Mother – who tinkled with her bear bell, dripped river water and loved chocolate – has become a ghost. Mum, who was as soft as a woolly jumper, who rose into the heights of the apple trees, and warmed clothes in the heat of the stove.

If only Dad would come back and tell his Lapland story again. If only he would talk about the Lovely Baby, who was born by means of an incision and almost made Dad himself faint. If only ordinary Mum would come back and invent a better ending for herself. If only she would tell stories properly and not add in too much of her own stuff. Without an ending, there's no story, but I don't want an ending like this.

# 6

When we lived at Extra Great Manor, I was the only girl at school with sheep and chandeliers at home. And a secret chamber, though not even my school friends knew about that. I was the Manor House Girl or the former Lovely Baby, and when the Manor House Girl had her tenth birthday, she pretended to have a ball with her friends. Auntie Annu lit the candles of the chandelier and poured juice in tall glasses for everyone. The Manor House Girl and her friends ran around upstairs, climbed into the room in the tower and stroked the sheep. Her friends said: 'You lead a strange life – your mum's dead and you've got fifteen bedrooms.' But they were too scared to go to the toilet by themselves. The toilet in the manor house was at the end of a long corridor. Auntie Annu had painted it dark red and hung framed black-and-white photos on the walls. One frame contained nothing but glass, under which you could see all twelve layers of wallpaper that had been found on the wall.

The Manor House Girl took her friends to the loo. They asked if she wasn't scared because there were so many empty rooms, but the Manor House Girl told them about a ghost hunter who had checked out the place before Auntie Annu had bought it. He had said that the house had a good atmosphere; Auntie bought it only after hearing that.

One of the girls switched off the lights in the toilet passage, and the Manor House Girl and her friends queued in the dark, in a small huddle. The ceiling creaked whenever Dad or Auntie Annu moved about upstairs. The Manor House Girl and her friends shrieked and laughed but they all did their weeing in the dark.

Then one day, Dad decided that we were going to move back to Sawdust House. For many years, he hadn't even glanced in the direction of the house whenever we had driven past, but all of a sudden, it was back to being an ordinary wooden house with breathing structures and the basics in order. All of a sudden, it had nothing whatsoever to do with Mum or her missing head or the hole in the veranda. Except that that, too, had been repaired. All of a sudden, Dad began talking about Mum in the past tense; all of a sudden, he was actually talking about Mum. All of a sudden, Dad began to build a patio, though earlier, he had said one wouldn't go with the Forties style.

No one had the sense to call a ghost hunter. 'The basic things are in order,' Dad assured me, and banged on his patio. How could he have known Mum had stayed on in Sawdust House, lying in wait? How could he have noticed such a thing, having talked Mum into the past tense?

And so Krista moved into Sawdust House, bringing her white furniture and clinking things with her. The clinking things included a beaded curtain, a glass jar filled with seashells, a porcelain angel, Chinese stress balls and a collection of glass bowls for tea lights.

Krista had only ever lived on her own, so all her things were women's things. She had a white sofa, a white table, an armchair and lots of decorative cushions with English slogans on them. She put up small, hand-painted signs above the towels in the bathroom, saying, *Hands*, *Guests* and *Bunnykins*. She enjoyed doing things like laying the table really nicely, lighting a candle, serving up the food and then taking a photo of the whole thing.

'Well, Saara, what does it feel like to move back into your own home?' Krista asked on moving day.

'Extra Great Manor was my home, too,' Manor House Girl replied.

'But, you know,' Krista went on, 'a person can have lots of different homes during the course of her life. I've had five as an adult. No, six, I mean.'

'Why did you have a double bed if you've always lived by yourself?' I asked.

'Saara,' Dad said, looking at me sternly.

'I was only asking.'

'We'll talk about it sometime later,' Dad said, which was his standard way of dealing with things he didn't want to talk about later.

'Hey, I bought a decoration for the door!' Krista cried. She took a beribboned, white-wicker door decoration out of her bag, which bore the words *Home Sweet Home*.

'I thought this might calm you down whenever you started worrying about mould or water damage.' Krista laughed, planting a kiss on Dad's cheek. Krista dared to laugh at Dad over all sorts of weird things.

Grown-ups are always asking what things feel like. But what answer can you give? This feels strange. When we came to Sawdust House for the first time to clean up and Dad asked me to get a bucket from the cleaning cupboard, I didn't even know where such a cupboard might be.

But on the other hand, as I stood there in the hall looking for the cleaning cupboard, I suddenly remembered clearly what our home smelled like when we came back from holiday. You don't smell home if you're there every day. But if you're away for a week, home acquires its own smell.

*This is what I smelled like when I was little.*

Perhaps houses and their inhabitants have that sort of connection: the house smells of its occupants and the occupants smell of their house. We exchanged smells when we moved to Extra Great Manor, and now I've got new, bigger clothes, and they all smell of high rooms, tile stoves and sheep's wool.


In the end, Dad came to get the bucket himself.

'Can't even ask for the smallest thing…' he muttered, going through the hall into the kitchen.

The cleaning cupboard wasn't in the hall. It was next to the food cupboard in the kitchen. Even the vacuum cleaner in the cupboard was a different colour from the one I'm sitting on in an old photo.

# 7

I'm woken up by the ghost. It's already sitting on the edge of my bed, pinning my hands down under the cover so they can't move. It doesn't look nasty or evil, just dead. Mum's ghost is looking at me but I can tell from its expression it doesn't recognize me.

It bends towards me and starts moving its lips. Its dark hair flops down in a familiar way. At first I only hear hissing, then I feel its breath.

My face is cold.

Then words come out. As if a radio were looking for a channel, the words have started but are hard to distinguish. Finally, I make out a whisper in the hissing:

'Snip! Snap! Snip!'

And after a while, again: 'Snip! Snap! Snip!'

I don't want to hear any more – I know what the words are. When I was little, Mum once borrowed *Struwwelpeter* from the library because she thought it was a funny book. But I was scared of *Struwwelpeter* and the book went back the following week. I was too frightened even to go near the H shelf, where *Struwwelpeter* lurked.

'Snip! Snap! Snip!' Mum whispers.

'Please don't,' I plead softly.

But Mum just goes on, clicking her scissors to the rhythm of the rhyme:

'The door flew open, in he ran,
The great, long, red-legg'd scissor-man.
Oh! children, see! the tailor's come
And caught out little Suck-a-Thumb.
Snip! Snap! Snip! the scissors go;
And Conrad cries out – Oh! Oh! Oh!
Snip! Snap! Snip! They go so fast,
That both his thumbs are off at last.'

The ghost turns to me, wielding the scissors. I hide my hands under my back and press my chin against the edge of the cover. The ghost looks for a way in under the bedclothes, its long hair swinging as it turns its head. Then it sits down on the floor by my bed, grips a corner of the cover and starts cutting a strip off the edge. The scissors click.

Snip, snap, snip, and the edge of the blanket comes loose.

'Too big,' the ghost croaks.

It seizes the blanket again and carries on cutting it into strips, this time along the upper edge. Snip, snap, snip, go the scissors under my chin.

The ghost crawls across my chest. I feel Mum's hair swipe my cheek.

'Too big,' the ghost mutters again. It turns at the corner and starts cutting a similar strip off the third edge.

When it turns to the fourth side, I pull my knees up to prevent the scissors touching my toes. Snip, snap, snip, it cuts off the lower edge.

Then it stops and turns towards my face. It looks at me for a moment, in the same blank way as before.

'Too big,' the ghostly voice says again.

Then it disappears, all of a sudden.

The chill gets in underneath the cover. I'm cold. I think of Bruno. His own mother tried to bite off his ear. I never did understand why. I don't understand this, either.

I lie quietly and wait. Mum doesn't come back; there's no clicking from the scissors. In Extra Great Manor, I could go inside a wall when I wanted to, but here, there's no room for anything like that. This is a healthy house with breathing structures, but that doesn't help.

# 8

I remember us eating the last jar of frozen strawberries labelled *2010* in Mum's handwriting. Auntie Annu had just emptied out the freezer of Sawdust House.

We ate the strawberries slowly. They were covered with a crisp layer of ice and sugar and they tasted wonderfully cold and sweet. No one talked about Mum's vegetable patch or about crushed ice or the veranda or the strawberry pyramid, which never got built once Dad's tyres had tumbled down the steps.

I remembered Mum's fingers were dyed crimson as she dropped berries into boxes. Pop, pop, went the plastic, and the sugar rasped on top. Mum licked her red fingers and ate the too-small strawberries herself. The strawberries that were too large she sliced in half with a knife. The knife was red with strawberry juice as well.

# 9

The kitchen is cold and filled with smoke. Krista's making pancakes. It's the morning of my birthday, and Krista has decided I am to have pancakes for breakfast. The window is open and the cooker fan is whirring away, but the whole of the downstairs is still full of smoke.

Wearing only her nightdress, Krista's freezing in front of the stove. That's why she's annoyed. As far as I'm concerned, she could stop cooking and go and get dressed, but Krista seems to think that birthday celebrations can only start once the pancakes are ready.

Krista's pancakes are thinner than real ones, and she only made a small amount of watery dough. She's prepared enough for us each to have two, though, really, the whole idea of pancakes is overindulgence. I miss Auntie Annu. Everything she did in the kitchen was big and splashy. She drove to the shop once a week and bought a huge amount of food. She cooked enough stew for three days in one go, and when she made pancakes, there was enough left over for a snack the following evening.

'Whipped cream on top! Otherwise it's not a proper birthday pancake!' Krista urges, plonking a spoonful of the stuff on to my pancake.

'I don't like it.'

'Try it! You'll see. Jam, too, and a mint leaf, and then I'll take a photo – wait!'

Krista fetches her phone and takes a picture of my pancake and cream. Then she writes underneath, *Happy Birthday, Saara!* and puts it out there.

Dad and Krista give me a hairdryer.

'This is from Annu,' Dad says, taking a roll of fabric out of the kitchen cupboard. 'She hid it here before she left. There should be a card inside.'

I undo the roll; it's a colourful rag rug.

In the depths of the rug, I find a card with a picture of an ancient-looking mosaic wall. The pattern shows a butterfly. The card says:

*Happy Birthday, sweetie! Do you remember these: your frog hoodie, purple cords, My Little Pony T-shirt, angel pyjamas? (I expect you recognize all the rest, too.) I thought it might be nice to keep the clothes as a souvenir – a bit like shells. Hey, now you are a real butterfly and twelve years old! Hugs and kisses! RunoutofroomA.*

'Will Auntie Annu ever come back to live at Extra Great Manor?' I ask.

'Who knows,' Dad mutters.

Dad's annoyed because after Auntie Annu disappeared, having gone out into the big wide world and started collecting stories, Extra Great Manor has become his responsibility. Winter's coming, the Blue Room has no wallpaper, no one has ordered logs for the winter and we don't even know what we should do with the sheep.

I look at the rug Auntie Annu wove. She was still in her square phase at that point. The rug is slightly longer than I am, and if I were to lie down in the middle of it and wrap it round myself, I could just fit inside, like a caterpillar in a cocoon.

The whole of my old wardrobe is in that rug, cut into even strips for the weft and slammed on the loom. The clothes I had when I moved to Extra Great Manor all that time ago. The rug has cotton stripes, denim stripes, frilly stripes and even two thin knicker stripes. It's got pink, orange, faded blue and green in it. A red raincoat glints here and there. I was quite a colourful girl back then. Fairly frilly, too.

Auntie Annu has sewn buttons and decorations braided from zips of different colours on the edges of the rug. The colours blending into one other make me think of water stirred in with oil. Everything is mixed up but I can still see each garment separately.

But the really amazing thing about the rug is the fact that it's so solid and compact, so even. Somehow Auntie Annu has managed to weave a clear-cut rectangle out of something that was so loose and flowing, so shrill and unreal. Both ends have been finished off, and the colours have been matched. There. It starts here and ends there. And that's the end of that.

I go upstairs. My new room has a blue-grey wooden floor. I can see the Wendy house and the veranda steps out of the window. Perhaps Dad doesn't want to sleep here because the window faces the garden steps. Mum's vegetable patch lies behind the steps, and Mum used to look out of this window first thing in the morning to see from the sky what kind of weather lay ahead.

I've got new curtains: blue butterflies on a white background.

I spread the birthday rug from Auntie Annu on the floor; it fits well there, almost as if she had guessed that one day the big upstairs bedroom would be mine. Almost as if my old clothes had known that one day they would be cut into strips and the floor would be blue-grey. Dad didn't even ask what room I wanted. He said I'd have my own space this way, and a bit of privacy, and put me upstairs. I didn't know I wanted my own space, a bit of privacy. The manor house had fifteen bedrooms; that was more than enough space.

I lie down on the new rug. I touch the green glimpse of the frog hoodie with my finger, and it answers greenly: croak. Good to see you.

# 10

The next time the ghost comes, it's carrying a carving knife. It sits down on the edge of my bed, as Mum used to do, and begins a story.

'Once upon a time, there were two sisters who wanted to get married,' the ghost rasps. 'The Prince came to test the shoe on them because he had decided that whomever the shoe fitted would marry him. The sisters wanted to have a go.'

The ghost's knife smells of sheep. Dad must have left it in the sink unwashed. I've spent the whole evening lying in my room, trying to block out the smell of roasting mutton that is oozing up the stairs. I can't believe they've killed Bruno.

' "Give the shoe here – I'll have a go!" said the first stepsister. She sat down to try it on.

'But her toes were too big. "Cut off the toe, cut off the toe," said the stepmother, and handed over a knife. "When you're Queen, you won't need to walk anyway."

'And the stepsister took the knife and cut off her big toe. She shoved her foot into the shoe and said, "It fits!" '

Apparently the knife is just a prop and the ghost doesn't plan on chopping anything off this time. It does choose to emphasize the 'It fits!' by raising the knife in the air, though.

'The Prince puzzled over the blood spurting out of the shoe and asked to have the shoe back.

'Then the other stepsister said, "Give the shoe here – I'll have a go!" And so she in turn sat down to try it on.

'This stepsister's heel was too big. Again, the stepmother handed over the knife and said, "Cut off the heel. When you're Queen, you won't need to walk anyway."

'And the other stepsister cut off her heel, shoved her foot into the shoe and said, "It fits!"

'But again the Prince puzzled over the blood spurting out of the shoe and asked to have the shoe back.

' "Give the shoe here!" said the first sister and cut off her foot. She shoved her leg stump into the shoe and said, "It fits!"

' "Give the shoe here!" said the second sister then, and cut off her own foot. She shoved her leg stump into the shoe and said, "It fits!"

' "Give the shoe here!" said the first sister then, and cut off her leg. She shoved her knee into the shoe and said, "It fits!"

' "Give the shoe here!" said the second sister then…

'When the sisters didn't have any legs left, the Prince took the blood-drenched shoe and left for the next house to look for the next girl. The sisters didn't get to marry. The end.'

The ghost waits for a moment, knife raised, pleased with itself. When I open my eyes, realizing the story has ended, it evaporates. I'm starving. I haven't eaten anything since coming home from school, because the kitchen table was strewn with blood-covered parcels of meat, but now my stomach hurts. I get up silently and creep downstairs.

I don't switch on the light as I go into the kitchen. I'm not scared of this house.

I take butter and cheese out of the fridge, and only then do I notice Krista standing by the window. She's looking out at the dark garden. She always looks so lost at night. As if she didn't remember why she was here and what house this was. Now she turns to look at me.

'Did you have a bad dream?' she asks.

I nod.

'Me, too,' she says.

Perhaps the ghost comes downstairs, too. What do I know? Perhaps everyone's got a ghost of their own. I look at Krista and wait to hear if she's going to say more. But she just turns back towards the window.

The dirty carving knife lies in the sink.

I butter three slices of bread and leave Krista in the dark.

Mum's things have been packed up into three large cardboard boxes and put in the attic. The first box contains official papers, two photo albums, bundles of letters tied together with yarn, a history of Auntie Brown, Auntie Marshmallow and Auntie Uncle's home village, Grandad's cap, Grandma's spoons, Mum's baby booties, a newspaper cutting about a pumpkin Auntie Brown grew, Mum's graduation cap and some old cups. Dad said that when I'm older, I can decide what to do with Mum's things, but until then, they can stay in the attic.

The other box contains Mum's clothes. Mum's party dress almost fits me now. On hangers, the clothes still looked alive, but when Dad took them down and folded them into flat piles, they died. I heard it. When Dad folded a big, grey, woolly jumper, I heard it expel its last breath before slumping.

The third box is full of shoes. Most of the shoes are still too big for me, but the mustard-coloured boots fit. They've got wooden heels and pointed toes, and they clatter when you walk in them. You can't mince or sprint – you can only take steady steps. Sometimes I put them on and walk to the shop and back. I love their echoing sound.

The ghost looks less and less like Mum each time it comes. What was familiar and Mum-like decreases; the ghost gets thinner and its weight on top of me gets lighter. Then it starts going haywire. As if it were no longer properly charged, it crackles and bounces and its stories get muddled. Maybe ghosts have batteries, and if they aren't charged, they go out in the end.

'*Once upon a time, there was a little sister who lost a key made out of a chicken bone,*' the ghost begins.

It always starts in the middle and chooses only the revolting bits. I know this bone bit; I try not to think about it every time we're eating chicken. Just as I try not to think about Bruno whenever the kitchen smells of rosemary.

'*What an idiot!*' the ghost snickers. '*Nothing for it but snip, snap, snip. What did you lose the key for? Hands up, who's got fingers? Ha, now it goes on, now it goes on. The little sister took a knife, cut off her little finger and opened the gate with it. And that's the end of that.*'

Auntie Annu always wanted to pull the wishbone. This involves two people gripping the bone with their little fingers and pulling till it snaps. The one who ends up with the bigger part can make a wish. I hated the snap and would have preferred not to pull. Also, Auntie had already won the lottery twice; she was hardly likely to need more wishes. If the bigger part did stay in my hand, as it sometimes did, I wished that Mum would send me a message. But she never did.

I don't see any need for a game that involves breaking bones.

The ghost clicks its fingers. First it tugs them, one at a time, then it clasps its hands together and crunches every joint. Mum never did that. It gives me a strange feeling of strength when I realize Mum didn't do that.

The ghost goes on with the story: *'A shepherd came and found the bone on the shore. He used it to whittle a mouthpiece for a horn.'*

'You already said that was the end.'

The ghost stops and looks at me.

'It's finished already,' I repeat.

*'Once upon a time, there was a horn,'* the ghost corrects itself, starting a new story. *'The shepherd blew the horn, and the bone began singing: "There's a girl inside the wall! It's murder, it's murder!" Her brothers heard the bone's song and opened up the wall. A maiden's skeleton slid out of the sawdust on to the floor. Only one bone was missing, the one that now sounded in the horn. The brothers went to their stepmother and asked, "What is the punishment for one who buries a maiden alive inside a wall?" And the stepmother replied, "Let such a villain be put inside a barrel*

*with sharp nails hammered into it and let him be rolled down a
mountainside to the water."*

' *"You have just pronounced your own sentence," the brothers
said, and shut the stepmother up in a barrel studded with nails.
Then they rolled her down a slope. Screaming horribly, the stepmother tumbled downwards before finally sinking into the water
beyond the edge of the land.'*

'You're not my mum,' I say to the ghost.

Two X-ray images hang on the wall in golden frames.
The first is of a shoulder. The second shows my teeth; that
was taken when I got a brace. I asked to have the picture
and demanded Dad got a golden frame for it to match the
first one.

I've got real bones in me. The ghost's joints click, but if a
doctor took an X-ray, it might not show anything. There are
teeth in me. Some of them still throb inside the gum because
they haven't got any room to grow. But they are there.

# 12

Then one day, when I come home from school, I hear Dad and Krista talking about Mum. I stay in the hall to listen. I want to know if they've seen the ghost.

'Maybe Hannele couldn't have died in any ordinary way,' Dad's voice says. 'She was such an unreal figure. As if she'd been plucked from a film. Maybe she needed a death like that.'

It's definitely Dad's voice. What on earth does he mean? Where's the bear bell, where's the chocolate? Mum didn't need any sort of death. What's he on about?

Dad and Krista are silent. Maybe Dad's now planting apologetic kisses on Krista's head. Still, he soon goes on: 'I have to say, it's better Hannele can't see the garden, given the state it's in. It's a jungle.'

My throat tightens. Is he really saying that it was better Mum died *so she didn't have to see the garden was a jungle*? The garden *would not be* a jungle if Mum were alive! The jungle came about because Dad spent a year in bed and then played hide-and-seek after that, driving past Sawdust House as if it didn't exist!

Dad has wrapped Mum in a parcel. Time has healed Dad and the fairy-tale characters are dead. Dad, who wept and wailed and filled the stove with *why why*, sits there now and is all like, oh yes, because it fitted in with the story.

Dad has put an end to Mum. He hasn't seen the ghost; he's been working on a patio and has decided that a lump of ice was a fitting end to Mum. He doesn't miss the bear bell because he's got Krista now, tinkling with her glass beads. If only the ghost would come with its scissors and cut his toes off.

At that very moment, a bang rings out from the living room. The whole house trembles and a pinch of sawdust sprays on to the floor. Without thinking, I open the kitchen door and go in. Inside the wall, something's rushing down.

Only then does my head fill with thoughts. Maybe a bird flew against the window. Maybe an elk bumped into the wall. Maybe the ghost toppled the bookcase over. Maybe something fell down from the sky again.

On the back wall of the living room, a half panel has blown open. There is a split in the wall; planks stick out in all directions and a big heap of sawdust has cascaded on to the floor. The trickling sawdust explains the rushing noise I heard in the hall. I stand there staring.

An apple tree is growing out of the split in the panel.

An apple tree.

Its slender stem pokes out of the panel. The trunk supports three branches with a few pale leaves on them. The seedling must have been growing inside the panel for a long time and gradually pressed itself against the top batten until finally it sprang like a bow and made the wall explode. The tree sticks up, greedily stretching towards the window.

I hear Dad moving in the bedroom; he appears at the kitchen door.

'Did you hear something, too?' Dad asks, before he sees the living-room wall. He stops in the doorway and stares.

'It's an apple tree,' I say.

Krista appears in the kitchen. Her belly is bare; she's rolled her trousers down and her top up. She covers her yawn with her hand.

Dad's still not saying a word. He scratches his head, taking deep breaths.

'How do you know it's an apple tree?' Krista asks.

'What does it matter whether it's an apple tree or not?' Dad shouts – more at himself than Krista.

'I don't know,' Krista answers, 'but…it's growing out of the wall.'

'From the leaves,' I reply. 'Apple trees have leaves like that.'

'But how can it be growing out of the wall?' Krista asks insistently.

I walk over to the tree. Sawdust sticks to my soles. I dodge the splinters shed by the planks and peer inside the panel. Tree roots slither behind the chipboard. They disappear into the depths of the floor. The sawdust is dark and damp, and an earthy smell drifts in.

The apple tree looks strong, though it's pale. I stroke its light stem. It must have grown from one of the seeds I pushed into the walls or the cracks in the floor as a little girl. It's been growing all these years.

I look at the wall. I remember the dirty wallpaper under the panel, with its pale shadows left behind by the furniture. This is the spot where Mum drew me one renovation day many years ago. Turquoise tights, pigtails and bobbles. I'm pretty sure this is the same spot.

Splinters, smashed planks, twisted nails. Perhaps Dad's right: growing up hurts.


Dad turns round and goes to make coffee. A short while after, the coffee machine starts bubbling, and he walks back into the living room, picks a loose piece of batten up off the floor and bends to inspect the wall. He pushes his hand inside, squeezes the sawdust he's grabbed and smells. He grabs another handful. This time, he's holding a handful of black, crumbling timber. He gasps for air and gulps; he glances at the edge of the ceiling, the window frame, the corner of the room.

'Phew. What now? I always…somehow I always.'

Dad squeezes the black crumbs of wood in his hand. He grips a plank visible through the hole and tugs; the rotten timber cracks like crispbread.

'Rainwater must have got in here. This is wet – the whole wall is wet. Wet and rotten…'

'What do we do now?' Krista asks.

'You mean with this wall?'

'And in general.'

'I don't know,' Dad answers. 'I really don't know.'

Then suddenly we hear a sob. Dad and I turn and see Krista standing in the middle of the floor. She stands there, helplessly far from any furniture, shivering.

'Help. Help me.' Krista's crying. She's pressing her hand against her mouth, looking as if she needed a chair or Dad or some other support.

'Rushing,' she sputters from behind her hand.

Dad goes to Krista, and just as he manages to put his arm around her, there's a splash inside Krista.

# 13

Sometimes, the end of the world comes. Sometimes, Paradise blasts out. Sometimes, someone dies so imperceptibly that there's no time to take it in. Perhaps a person like that will try to come back as a ghost to continue her interrupted stories. Though you should really just make your exit. You should stop by the roadside and let the car go. You should become black and white. You should shrink and change your tense.

Perhaps our family's endings are always bad. Perhaps that's why we liked watching the Belgian detective at work. He would have been sure to complete the renovations, finish all the bedtime stories, visit Auntie Marshmallow and explain each death properly. His plots had nothing superfluous about them, and his clothes fitted perfectly – no room to grow there. He would have written a letter and left it in a suitably obvious place.

He was always elegant and tip-top. He had one question and one answer. His shoulders stayed in their sockets and his toes didn't go missing.

But we just stand here. We watch and we wait. Krista leaks seawater; Dad claws at the rotten wall; the coffee machine hums. Will someone call us into the library? Will someone put all this into a gold frame? Or is it enough that the doctor gives a yank and fingers move again?

The world goes on. Nothing becomes clear, but time heals and people forget. The ghost's batteries run out. Things happen. Overlapping, at the wrong time, at different times, in the wrong places. The angels aren't in control. Because there's always bound to be someone who forgets to listen to the news, looks even though they shouldn't, or stands in the wrong place.

And that's the end of that.

## Oneworld, Many Voices

Bringing you exceptional writing
from around the world

*Umami* by Laia Jufresa (Spanish)
Translated by Sophie Hughes

*The Hermit* by Thomas Rydahl (Danish)
Translated by K. E. Semmel

*The Peculiar Life of a Lonely Postman* by Denis Thériault
(French) Translated by Liedewy Hawke

*Three Envelopes* by Nir Hezroni (Hebrew)
Translated by Steven Cohen

*Fever Dream* by Samanta Schweblin (Spanish)
Translated by Megan McDowell

*The Invisible Life of Euridice Gusmao* by Martha Batalha
(Brazilian Portuguese) Translated by Eric M. B. Becker

*The Temptation to Be Happy* by Lorenzo Marone
(Italian) Translated by Shaun Whiteside

*Sweet Bean Paste* by Durian Sukegawa (Japanese)
Translated by Alison Watts

*They Know Not What They Do* by Jussi Valtonen (Finnish)
Translated by Kristian London

*The Tiger and the Acrobat* by Susanna Tamaro (Italian)
Translated by Nicoleugenia Prezzavento and Vicki Satlow

*The Woman at 1,000 Degrees* by Hallgrímur Helgason
(Icelandic) Translated by Brian FitzGibbon

*Frankenstein in Baghdad* by Ahmed Saadawi (Arabic)
Translated by Jonathan Wright

*Back Up* by Paul Colize (French)
Translated by Louise Rogers Lalaurie

*Damnation* by Peter Beck (German)
Translated by Jamie Bulloch

*Oneiron* by Laura Lindstedt (Finnish)
Translated by Owen Witesman

*The Baghdad Clock* by Shahad Al Rawi (Arabic)
Translated by Luke Leafgren

---

*The Aviator* by Eugene Vodolazkin (Russian)
Translated by Lisa C. Hayden

---

*Lala* by Jacek Dehnel (Polish)
Translated by Antonia Lloyd-Jones

---

*Bogotá 39: New Voices from Latin America*
(Spanish and Portuguese) Short story anthology

---

*Last Instructions* by Nir Hezroni (Hebrew)
Translated by Steven Cohen

---

*Solovyov and Larionov* by Eugene Vodolazkin (Russian)
Translated by Lisa C. Hayden

---

*In/Half* by Jasmin B. Frelih (Slovenian)
Translated by Jason Blake

---

*What Hell Is Not* by Alessandro D'Avenia (Italian)
Translated by Jeremy Parzen

---

*Zuleikha* by Guzel Yakhina (Russian)
Translated by Lisa C. Hayden

---

*Mouthful of Birds* by Samanta Schweblin (Spanish)
Translated by Megan McDowell

---

*City of Jasmine* by Olga Grjasnowa (German)
Translated by Katy Derbyshire

---

*Things that Fall from the Sky* by Selja Ahava (Finnish)
Translated by Emily Jeremiah and Fleur Jeremiah

---

*Mrs Mohr Goes Missing* by Maryla Szymiczkowa (Polish)
Translated by Antonia Lloyd-Jones

---

*In the Shadow of Wolves* by Alvydas Šlepikas (Lithuanian)
Translated by Romas Kinka

---

*Humiliation* by Paulina Flores (Spanish)
Translated by Megan McDowell

# ONEWORLD TRANSLATED FICTION PROGRAMME

Co-funded by the
Creative Europe Programme
of the European Union

**IN/HALF by Jasmin B. Frelih**
Translated from the Slovenian by Jason Blake
Publication date: November 2018 (UK & US)

**WHAT HELL IS NOT by Alessandro D'Avenia**
Translated from the Italian by Jeremy Parzen
Publication date: January 2019 (UK & US)

**CITY OF JASMINE by Olga Grjasnowa**
Translated from the German by Katy Derbyshire
Publication date: March 2019 (UK) / April 2019 (US)

**THINGS THAT FALL FROM THE SKY by Selja Ahava**
Translated from the Finnish by Emily and Fleur Jeremiah
Publication date: April 2019 (UK) / May 2019 (US)

**MRS MOHR GOES MISSING by Maryla Szymiczkowa**
Translated from the Polish by Antonia Lloyd-Jones
Publication date: March 2019 (UK)

Oneworld's award-winning translated fiction list is dedicated to publishing
the best contemporary writing from around the world, introducing readers
to acclaimed international writers and brilliant, diverse stories. With these
five titles from across Europe, generously supported by the Creative
Europe programme as well as various in-country literary and cultural
organizations, we are continuing to break boundaries and to bring new
and exciting voices into English for the first time.

For the latest updates, visit oneworld-publications.com/creative-europe